Abby Carnelia's
One & Only
Magical Power

Abby Carnelia's One & Only Magical Power

by David Pogue

Roaring Brook Press New York

Text copyright © 2010 by David Pogue
Jacket illustration copyright © 2010 by Antonio Caparo
Published by Roaring Brook Press
Roaring Brook Press is a division of
Holtzbrinck Publishing Holdings Limited Partnership
175 Fifth Avenue, New York, New York 10010
www.roaringbrookpress.com

Distributed in Canada by H. B. Fenn and Company Ltd.

Library of Congress Cataloging-in-Publication Data

Pogue, David, 1963–
    Abby Carnelia's one and only magical power / David Pogue. — 1st ed.
      p. cm.
    Summary: After eleven-year-old Abby discovers that she has a completely useless magical
power, she finds herself at a magic camp where her hope of finding others like herself is
realized, but when a select group is taken to a different camp, a sinister plot comes to light.
    ISBN: 978-1-59643-384-7
    [1. Magic—Fiction. 2. Camps—Fiction. 3. Ability—Fiction. 4. Family life—
Connecticut—Fiction. 5. Connecticut—Fiction.] I. Title.
    PZ7.P75163Abb 2010
    [Fic]—dc22   2009046619

First Edition May 2010

Printed in March 2010 in the United States of America by
RR Donnelley & Sons Company, Harrisonburg, Virginia

1   3   5   7   9   8   6   4   2

For Kelly, Tia, and Jeffrey,
who make me believe in magic every single day.

Contents

CHAPTER
1
Egg

YOU'VE PROBABLY SEEN THE ADS for Abby Carnelia's Find-Your-Magic Centers on TV. Or maybe you've seen a Find-Your-Magic Center at the shopping mall, tucked in between the Gap and the drugstore. But Abby Carnelia herself didn't discover her own magical power until she was eleven years old.

This is how it happened.

One Saturday in April, Abby and her little brother, Ryan, were in the kitchen, helping their mom make a chef's salad for lunch. Mrs. Carnelia's version of the chef's salad was basically a big tossed salad with sliced-up ham, turkey, bacon, eggs, and sometimes leftovers from the fridge that really had no business being in a salad.

Ryan was setting the table. Abby was slicing up the hard-boiled eggs. Mrs. Carnelia walked by with a piece of meatloaf that was about to become salad topping.

"Did you lose an earring, honey?" she asked. "Or are you just going for a lopsided look?"

Abby looked up from the eggs. "What?"

"You're missing an earring."

Abby's hands automatically went up to her earlobes. Sure enough, she could feel the left aquamarine earring still in place. But on the right side, there was nothing but a naked, rubbery, pierced earlobe.

On any other day, she might have run upstairs to look for the other earring, or felt around on the floor, or tried to remember putting them on.

And on any other day, she might have heard any of the three things that people in that kitchen said next. First came Ryan's wisecrack: "It probably fell in the salad. Chew slowly, people." (Ryan was eight. Wisecracks were his specialty.)

Then came her mother's question: "Are you sure you put it on today, honey?"

Then her dad boomed into the kitchen, big and bald. "And good morrow to you, my beetlings!"

(He always said stuff like that. And no, I don't know what "beetlings" means, either. It's just what he had

always called his kids for as long as Abby could remember.)

But this was not any normal day, and Abby didn't hear
anything. She was too busy looking at the egg. Staring at
it, actually, with just about the weirdest expression you've
ever seen on a sixth grader's face.

It was a hard-boiled egg. Just a plain white chicken's egg,
like every egg you've ever seen. There was only one thing
unusual about it: this egg was spinning. Slowly, sitting there on
the counter, turning around and around.

Now, in itself, a spinning egg isn't especially freaky. In the
history of the world, there have probably been thousands
of spinning eggs. There are egg-spinning science experiments, egg-spinning games, and probably world records
for spinning eggs. What made this particular spinning egg
so unusual was that nothing had touched it. Nothing had come
anywhere near it. There are very few world records for eggs
that start spinning all by themselves, for no reason.

Abby, frowning hard at that egg, reached out to stop it
with her hand. There. Now it was sitting still, just like an egg
is supposed to.

But then a little voice in her head seemed to say: Try it
again! So for the second time, Abby Carnelia reached up
and tugged at her earlobes, just like she had the first time
she checked for the missing earring.

And there it was: the egg started spinning again. By itself.

She was speechless. Even the little voice in her head was speechless.

She stopped the egg again. She tugged her earlobes again. It started spinning again. Always slowly, always the same direction, and always perfectly evenly, without any of the wobble you'd get if you spun an egg with your hand.

Now, Abby loved science. She had spent two years in Brownies, knew how to make a few recipes (which is science, after all), and had been the only girl in fifth grade not to be grossed out when they dissected a frog in science class.

She knew all the basic laws of science, like "What goes up must come down" and "Nature abhors a vacuum." But she had never heard the one that goes, "Eggs spin when you pull on your ears."

Abby's mom repeated her question. "Abby? Are you sure you put on both earrings this morning?"

It was Ryan, though, who first realized that something was going on. He trotted over to see what Abby was looking at. And he saw the egg start spinning by itself.

"WHOA, DUDE!" he said.

Abby came back to earth, noticed him there, and stopped the egg. She picked it up and tapped it on the bowl to crack its shell, ready to peel it, as though nothing had happened.

"What, Ry?" said their mom.

"Abby just did the coolest trick. Do it again!"

But Abby was confused and just a little bit freaked out. A thousand thoughts were crowding her brain, and her stomach was doing the jitterbug.

So she pretended that nothing was going on. She finished peeling the egg and began to slice it. "I was just fooling around," she managed. "Forget it."

Of course, you can't tell an excited eight-year-old boy to forget anything.

"No, c'mon! Do it again!"

Ryan grabbed another hard-boiled egg himself and tried to make it spin the way Abby had. He waved his hands around it. He blew on it. He made ghost noises with his mouth.

"What did you do, blow on it? I bet you blew on it. Show Mom. Mom! Come here! Look at Abby's egg trick! Hey, Dad! Want to see something cool? Abby did a trick!"

Abby rolled her eyes. "It's nothing, all right? It's just a stupid egg."

5

But her parents had now joined her at the counter.

"No egg is stupid," proclaimed her dad. "Bring forth the trick with all due speed!"

"I'd love to see it, hon," added her mother.

"Doooooo IT! Dooooo IT! Dooooo IT!" chanted Ryan.

Abby, flustered, didn't know what to do. She had already sliced up the first egg; it was salad bits at this point. She had no idea if a different egg would work.

Ryan grabbed another one from the bowl, set it on the counter, and flicked at it with his pointer finger. "Do the thing, Abby!"

The little voice in her head said: *Oh, go ahead. Just do the thing.*

Abby nervously pushed her long, dark brown hair back over her shoulders. She steadied this new egg with her hand. Then, as her family watched, she tugged her earlobes.

The egg began to spin by itself. It kept spinning as long as she kept tugging.

"WICKED!" shouted Ryan. "How do you blow it from so far away? No, I know. It's a magnet! Can I try? Where's the magnet? Lemme try!"

"That's great, honey," said Mrs. Carnelia, giving Abby's shoulders an affectionate squeeze. "You sure have me fooled!" And she walked away to pour the milk.

Only Abby's father said nothing. And for him to say nothing was highly unusual. He had a feeling that there was more to this than just a spinning hard-boiled egg.

And, as everyone knows by now, he was absolutely right.

CHAPTER
2
Magic

THINK ABOUT EVERY MOVIE you've ever seen where something magical or impossible happens. *Cinderella. Peter Pan. Freaky Friday. The Shaggy Dog. Dr. Dolittle. Lilo & Stitch. Aladdin. Alvin and the Chipmunks. Aquamarine. The Lion, the Witch, and the Wardrobe. Chitty Chitty Bang Bang. The Indian in the Cupboard. Nanny McPhee. Sky High. Night at the Museum.* And, of course, about 67,000 superhero movies. What do they all have in common?

In every one of these movies, something happens that breaks the laws of nature. Animals talk, cars fly, people get superpowers, whatever.

And how do the characters react? They say "Wow!" their faces light up in astonishment, and they talk about it for four seconds. And then they move on with the story.

Hello! *Four seconds?*

In fiction, they say: "Hey, you turned that pumpkin into a carriage. Awesome. Let's get in and go to the ball!"

But if something like that really happened—if it happened to YOU, you would talk about it for more than four seconds. You would FREAK OUT. You'd be thinking, "Holy jeez!! I've just seen a violation of the laws of nature that have controlled the world for oh, I don't know, about 4.5 billion years! That's insane! Actually, maybe I'm insane because such a thing has never, ever happened before! Surely I'm mistaken! Breathe. Breathe. Take it slow. Seek professional help. Ask your doctor if psychotherapy is right for you."

Then you'd tell everyone you knew. You wouldn't be able to shut up about it. You'd go on TV shows. You'd write a book. You'd set up a Web site!

So maybe you can understand why Abby, a real-world person, pretty much splatted onto the ceiling.

See, Abby liked her life, her family, and her friends. She even liked school pretty well. But sometimes she just felt so . . . average. Average height, average singing voice, average looks. Eventually, when the kids in her class grew up, Abby doubted very much that anyone would look back and remember her.

Yes, she was an okay artist, did fine with her grades, was

coming along on her clarinet. She had a Web page, a blog called Abbylog, which she updated twice a week, and which had an audience of six people (plus her parents, who don't really count). That was something, at least. Oh, and she could fold her eyelids inside out, which was primarily useful in grossing out Ryan to make him stop bugging her.

But she couldn't charm the teachers with a toss of blond hair like Tiffany Sykes. She hadn't been in a TV commercial like Amber Jessup. And nobody fought over her when they were picking players for teams, like they did over Stacia Dornfeld.

That didn't mean *nobody* thought she was special. Her mom thought she was, but of course moms are required to think that. Her dad always said that she was a "diamond in the rough" and that someday the world would "beat a path to her door." But all of that future-potential stuff didn't make Abby special *now*.

This, though, was different. Abby couldn't help wondering if maybe this egg thing was *really* special. Made *her* special. Well, okay, maybe not special, but at least unusual. She was pretty sure that if someone invented a sport someday where you got points for spinning farm-fresh poultry products without touching them, they'd pick her before they picked Stacia Dornfeld.

Besides, said the little voice in Abby's head, *maybe the egg thing is only the beginning.*

That little voice couldn't stop asking questions. *What does it mean? Am I a witch? Have I always had this power? Is this only the first miracle of many? Will I develop new powers later? What else can I move with my mind—I mean, with my earlobes? Are there actual schools for real wizards?*

How do you set up a Web site?

Months later, Ryan and Mrs. Carnelia would both swear that Abby did, in fact, eat a plate of chef's salad that afternoon. But if you ask her today, she'll say she doesn't remember it. She just remembers counting the seconds until she could run up to her room and make some more magic.

Amber Jessup may have had her 30 seconds of fame on TV. But Abby Carnelia, the world's first *actual* person to have magic? That was huge. She'd be the first eleven-year-old to have her own TV show. No, wait—her own channel!

After lunch, she nearly threw her plates in the sink, muttered something to her mom in a hurry (it sounded like "thanksforlunchMomI'llbereadinginmyroomBye") and flew upstairs.

Of course, reading wasn't what Abby had in mind. She closed her door, pulled out the two hard-boiled eggs she had slipped into her sweater pocket, and prepared to blow her own mind.

She set the eggs on her bedside table, sat cross-legged on her purple bedspread, and began running some tests.

Would an egg spin if she tugged on only one earlobe? No, it had to be both of them.

Would the egg spin if she closed her eyes? No, she had to be looking at it. That's how she controlled which egg would spin.

Could she make the egg spin in the other direction? No, always clockwise.

Could she control the speed of the spinning? No. It was always that slow, steady spinning.

Could she make anything else spin? She tried a super-ball . . . a Nerf football . . . her toothbrush . . . a hair scrunchie . . . nothing. Right after lunch, Abby had been high as a kite. Her imagination had run wild with the limitless possibilities of being the only person on earth with *real magic*. Fame! Fortune! Blogs!

But the more she experimented, the more the crushing truth began to sink in: this was it.

Only eggs. Only earlobes. Only spinning.

Only NOTHING, said the sarcastic little voice in her head.

Finally, defeated, Abby crashed onto her pillow. She rubbed her face unhappily. What good was magic if this was all it could do? What's the point of magic if you can't control what it does, or at least make it do something useful? Who cares if you have magic if you can't make things float and change and turn invisible, or command animals to do your bidding, or make people like Tiffany Sykes spill soda on their clothes at lunch?

Abby's magical power was—the little voice in her head wouldn't stop saying it—*stupid*. She had a stupid magical power.

The sheer randomness and pointlessness of her power drove Abby crazy. Her trick was so trivial; nobody around her even recognized it as supernatural.

Her family just thought it was a cheesy magic trick. Ryan's latest theory involved invisible threads. And when Abby asked her mother what she thought of her egg trick, the response was: "I think it's terrific, hon. Now see if you can magically clean up your room."

Sigh.

Finally, she couldn't take it anymore; she felt that if she didn't tell *someone*, she'd explode. So at lunch on Monday, Abby grabbed her best friend, Morgan, by the elbow just as they were leaving the cafeteria line.

"Sit with me at the nut-free table," she whispered. "It's important."

"What for?" Morgan whispered back. "And why are we whispering?"

Abby and Morgan almost always sat together at

lunch—they'd been friends since first grade—but never at the nut-free table. Nobody sat at the table for kids with nut allergies, except kids with nut allergies. On most days, there were only two or three kids sitting there at a table designed for ten.

"Trust me," Abby said. She grabbed her tray and led the way.

They sat down at the far end of the nut-free table. Abby pulled the hard-boiled egg out of her lunch bag.

"Okay, hold out your hand flat," she said.

Morgan held her hand out. Abby set the egg down on Morgan's palm.

"Keep it like that. Don't move. I'm not going to touch this egg, or blow, or anything."

She made it spin in Morgan's hand.

"Dang, dawg!" said Morgan, drawing her head backward, her green eyes wide. "That is a *rockin'* magic trick!"

Then Morgan closed her hand on the egg to make it stop spinning. She studied it closely.

"Okay, I give up. How do you do it?"

Abby looked her straight in the eye.

"It's not a trick, Morgan," she said intensely. "It's a *power*."

Morgan looked around the cafeteria, half to see who else might be watching, and half to get her thoughts together.

"Yo, girl," she said quietly. "I'm sorry, but there's no

such thing as powers. I'm supposed to believe that you're making that egg spin with your mind?"

"Not my mind! With my earlobes," Abby said. Morgan started getting up to leave, and Abby suddenly realized how silly that sounded. "I mean, I don't really know *how* I'm doing it. It does it."

"Can you move stuff around? Maybe you have that ESP thing where you can move stuff around with mind control!"

Abby shook her head. "I spent all weekend trying. This is it. This is all I can do. My one and only magical power."

Morgan sipped her diet soda thoughtfully. "Well, if that's really a magical power, it's a pretty lame one," she said finally. "Wouldn't it be better if you could fly? Or turn invisible? Or, like, make Mrs. Thatch forget the names of the state capitals?"

Abby threw her head back in exasperation. "Yes, I know. Don't you think I'd rather have powers like that? But this is it. It is what it is."

"Well, if you're telling me the truth," Morgan said finally, "then I think you should find out more about this. Get some books from the library. Google it."

Abby nodded; that was good advice. Surely there was somebody, somewhere, at some time in history, who had made an egg spin and written about it.

"Okay, gimme the egg," she told Morgan.

"How come?" Morgan asked, handing it over.

"Because it's not just a trick," Abby began. "It's—"

"I know, I know, it's a power," Morgan interrupted, grinning.

"No," said Abby. "It's my lunch."

CHAPTER

3

Library

ONE OF THE PERKS OF LIVING in a leafy suburb like East-port is that you can pretty much ride your bike anywhere. Most of the streets even have sidewalks, so your parents don't flip out when you say you're going to ride your bike to the library.

That's exactly what Abby planned to do after school. Her dad offered to drive her, but Morgan was going to meet her at the library, and Abby didn't want a hovering adult hanging over them.

"No, thanks," she told him on her way out. "It's such a beautiful day, I think I'll ride my bike. You know, get some fresh air and exercise."

Ryan had just burst into the kitchen. He stared at her as

though she'd grown antlers. "You want to get fresh air and exercise?"

"Leave me alone, Ryan. I'm going to the library with Morgan. Bye, Dad!" She pushed open the door to the garage.

But Ryan scampered right along after her.

"Wait, wait! Before you go—do this one!"

He waved a piece of scrap paper under her nose.

"Ryan, *please*. I gotta go, okay? Let's do your code later."

Ryan had become obsessed with codes lately. He'd filled a hundred pieces of scrap paper with nonsensical-looking writing that, once you solved it, always turned out to be some eight-year-old's idea of a joke, like "Q: What do you get when you cross a snowman with a vampire? A: FROSTBITE."

"Oh, *come on*, Ab! *Pleeeeeease?* Please please please please please? Just real quick!"

Abby sighed loudly to make her point. Then she turned and grabbed the piece of paper from Ryan's hand. She read what was written there in his cramped little pencil writing:

Your time has come to leave. Fly away! Is evil going to prevail? Open the door and flee!

Abby had twenty minutes to get to the library and meet Morgan. "It's a masterpiece, Ryan. Too hard for me. I give up." She tried to hand the paper back to him.

"No, no!" said Ryan, "Find the hidden message! Okay, I'll give you a hint. It's a first-word code. Just read the first words of the sentences."

Abby looked at it again, reading the first words out loud. "Your . . . fly . . . is . . . open."

Ryan clapped his hands and cackled hysterically.

"Cute. Real cute," she told him. "Hey, when we both grow up and become spies, you'll be the first person I'll communicate with. And that's a promise." She reached out and ruffled his hair, then turned to get her bike.

"Wait, wait! I have to teach you the second-word code!"

"When I come back, Ry. See ya!"

Little brothers, Abby thought as she strapped on her bike helmet. *Can't live with 'em, can't sell 'em on eBay.*

The Eastport Public Library, ten blocks from the Carnelias' house, is a very modern library—the pride of Eastport. You can borrow DVD movies, music CDs, computer game cartridges, gadgets like iPods or GPS things for your car—you can even check out toys. Some people claim that somewhere in the back, the Eastport Public Library even has *books.*

"Yo, girl," said Morgan when Abby arrived. "You ready for some hardcore Googling? Let's do this thing."

Once inside the library, they each bought a bottle of

iced tea (the Eastport Library had had a café since 1998) and sat down by the computers to search the Internet.

Abby fired up Google and tried typing in phrases like "spinning egg magic."

That search led her to all kinds of science videos, all very interesting. "Dude! Look at this!" she whispered to Morgan.

They watched a YouTube video that showed how you can spin a *boiled* egg on its end—you know, standing up—but a *raw* egg just falls over when you try.

"I got one, too. Look at this," Morgan whispered back. She pointed to her own screen, where Abby read an article about crushing eggs with your hand. She learned that it's really hard to crush an egg when your hand is wrapped all the way around it; the shell distributes the force evenly, even if you squeeze really hard.

On a Web site about science magic, they found out that you can make an entire hard-boiled egg scoot out of its shell just by blowing on it really hard—if, beforehand, you just make a pinhole in one end and a dime-sized hole at the far end.

At one point, Morgan rapped Abby excitedly on the shoulder. "Dawg—this is it! This is your trick!"

Abby scooted her chair over. Morgan hit Play. It was a video of somebody spinning an egg with his hand, then stopping it briefly with his finger—and when he took his hand away, the egg started spinning again.

Abby and Morgan looked at each other. It was *so* close!

But that's when the narrator popped onto the screen. It was one of those Mr. Science–type guys, with stick-out ears and a white lab coat.

"Magic? Of course not!" he was saying. "Remember: there's no such thing as magic! There's only science. What we're showing you now is just a cool feature of regular eggs. Once you start spinning an egg, the momentum of all that yolky stuff inside wants to keep going—even if you stop it for a second with your finger. But you don't have to tell your friends that; I won't mind!"

Abby softly banged her forehead on the keyboard.

After half an hour, Abby and Morgan gradually reached an astonishing conclusion: in the entire, massive, pulsing Internet universe, there was not one single Web page about making an egg spin by pulling your earlobes.

"Okay then," said Morgan matter-of-factly. She stood up. "We'll try books."

As it turned out, most of what the library had were magic books—books full of magic *tricks*. They rounded up a few of those to check out, just to get a feel for the field.

There were also a few books about *real* magic, with titles

like *Witches, Warlocks, and Wizardry: Magic Belief Systems Through History* and *The Human Need for Magic: A Sociological Approach.* Abby's interest perked up; maybe these books would be more like it.

By the time Abby said goodbye to Morgan and rode home, there were eleven books in her backpack. Most of them were hardcover books, and they were heavy. It took her longer to ride her bike back from the library than it had taken her to get there.

After a week of disappearing into her library books, Abby reached what she thought were two important conclusions about magic.

First, people have always wished that magic were real. The first civilizations worshiping the sun and the stars . . . the Greeks with their mythology of magical gods . . . people these days who pay to see magicians who they know are faking it—everybody wants to believe that magic is possible.

Second, people usually find out eventually that there is no real magic.

Oh, there are close calls. There are all kinds of things that people want to believe in. There are freaky coincidences, rumors, and ancient tales of mysticism from centuries ago.

There are religious miracles that nobody's ever seen first-hand.

But when it comes to magic that you can see yourself, repeat reliably, prove scientifically, there's never been much of anything.

Until I came along, Abby thought with mixed emotions.

One night, she was sitting on her bed, flipping through the last chapters of *Sorcery and Society: The Need to Believe,* when a voice boomed from her doorway.

"Pardon the intrusion, my little Abbitha. Do I disturb?"

She looked up to see her father's grinning face.

"No, no, come on in," she said.

It was hard to resist Mr. Carnelia. He had a gentle soul, he had little nicknames for everyone, and he made the best spaghetti sauce ever.

Or at least he did when he was around. In those days, he worked as an airline pilot. And airline pilots have some of the wackiest work schedules in the world: they're away from home for twenty days in a row, flying around the country, and then they're home for two weeks straight. Abby liked the dad-at-home weeks a lot more than the dad-not-there weeks.

"Doing some homework, are we?" he said as he sat down on her stuffed-animal trunk.

"Yeah," Abby lied. "Just some school stuff."

He raised his eyebrows. "Homework about witch doctors and Houdini?"

He nudged a book on the floor with his foot. It was called The Focus on Hocus Pocus. On the cover, there were pictures of magicians through the ages.

"What kind of school do we send you to, anyway?"

Abby sighed and flopped back on her pillows. "Okay, it's not really school homework," she said.

Mr. Carnelia bent over, picked up the book, and walked over to sit on the foot of her bed.

"Now listen, little one," he said kindly. "You don't get to be as old as I am without learning how to tell when something is on your favorite daughter's mind."

He tapped her ankle gently twice with his meaty fist. "You rush off from dinner every night, you haven't written anything on your blog in two weeks, and we've almost forgotten what Morgan looks like. Something is up with you, beetling."

Abby scrunched farther down into her pillows.

"I'm going to stick my neck out here," he went on, "and make a guess. I believe that all of this has something to do with what happened the other day to your hard-boiled egg. Am I close?"

Abby just turned over onto her stomach, face in the pillows.

"I'll take that as a yes," he said. "Well, in that case, I'll let you in on a little secret: I don't believe in magic myself. But I do believe in Abigail the Magnificent. And I would like to become your patron."

"What's that?" Abby allowed one eye to peek out from the pillow folds.

"In the golden age, my dear, there were great musicians and artistes, and then there were the patrons—the rich and the royals, who gave money to those performers and creators to support their artistic endeavors."

Abby flopped back over to look at him, listening carefully.

"What you may not realize, little McAbbister, is that I was once quite a magician myself. I pulled enough quarters out of ears to fill the Grand Canyon. I did amateur birthday party shows for every kid who ever turned six in Bernard, Oregon. And it's quite apparent that you, my dear, have been bitten by the magic bug."

Half of Abby wanted to reply, *Well, kind of.* And the other half wanted to say, *Well, not really. I don't want to perform—I just want to know what's going on with me!*

She couldn't decide whether or not to discuss her powers with her dad. He was the most understanding adult she'd ever met, but he was still an adult.

In the end, she didn't have to say anything. He reached

into his back pocket and carefully unfolded something he'd torn out of the newspaper.

"So I wanted to show you this," he said. "I saw it and I thought of you right away."

She took the clipping from him and examined it. It was an ad. It said:

"*Magic camp?*" said Abby.

"It's only a thought," smiled her dad. "But if I may say so, it's a brilliant thought. Magic camp changed my whole life."

"You went to magic camp?"

"Indeed," he replied. "When I was thirteen. It was my first sleep-away camp, and it was unforgettable. Professional magicians would come to perform at night, and we'd work on our tricks all day. I made friends that I'm still in touch with to this very day."

"But I don't know any magic tricks," Abby blurted before she could stop herself.

Mr. Carnelia eyed her carefully.

"Abster. I have seen you do positively alarming things to a Grade A chicken's egg. I have seen you cover your bedroom carpeting with enough magic books to fill a library. You can't tell me that you don't know any magic."

The thing was, some of those books really *had* gotten Abby sort of interested in the whole hobby. And there was something in the newspaper ad that had really gotten her attention: that bit about "unexplained phenomena." If ever there was an unexplained phenomenon, earlobe egg spinning was it.

"Isn't it going to be all boys?" Abby asked.

"Well, if it *is* mostly boys, you're getting to the age where that might actually be considered a bonus." He got up from the bed. "But I'll tell you what. I'll try to find out more about this place, and you give it some thought for this summer. What say ye?"

He offered his hand. Abby grinned and stuck out her foot for him to shake.

"Deal," she said.

She didn't know it at the time, but magic camp was going to be a very big deal indeed.

CHAPTER
4
Pool

"**M**AGIC CAMP?" RYAN SHOUTED. "She gets to go to magic camp? Don't tell me it's sleep-away camp!"

Abby smiled at him sweetly. "It's sleep-away camp."

"Mom!" said Ryan, annoyed.

"Abby's eleven, honey," his mother replied. "When you're eleven, you can go to sleep-away camp, too."

They were sitting at a white metal table beside the town pool, drying off. Camp Cadabra's brochure had come in the mail—if you could call it a brochure. It was more like a glossy magazine, sixty-four pages long. It had page after page of gorgeous photos, showing kids laughing in the sunshine, sailing on a rippling blue lake, and practicing magic tricks with brightly colored silk scarves in a sunlit outdoor theater.

Mrs. Carnelia shook her head. "Besides, honey, nothing's for sure yet. I'm not sure we could send Abby to this camp even if we wanted to. It looks like a camp for millionaires. And we are definitely not millionaires."

"Well, how much is it?" Abby asked. "Maybe I could just go for the two-week session."

Two months ago, magic camp would have been the last thing on Abby's wish list. There were plenty of other camps that would have come first in her mind: music camp, art camp, maybe lying-on-the-beach-with-milkshakes-reading camp. Magic camp never would have occurred to her.

But that was before she discovered that she was a freak.

That was before she'd changed, in her own mind, from Abby the Average to Abby the Truly Weird. And at this point, after exhausting all hope of finding out more about her weirdness online and in books, this camp thing was looking like her best hope at getting some professional advice. The more she'd thought about it, and listened to her dad's great funny stories from his magic-camp days, and looked at those pictures in the brochure—the more she wanted to go.

As she rooted around in the white mailing envelope that had brought the Camp Cadabra brochure, Mrs. Carnelia made a discovery. "Aha!" she said, pulling out a white piece of paper. "The price list."

Abby knew that her family didn't have a ton of money. She looked out at the sunshine sparkling on the town pool, watched some kid jumping off the diving board, and prepared herself for the bad news.

"Good heavens! How could anyone afford to go to a camp this expensive?" she imagined her mom saying.

But that's not what her mom actually said.

"Good heavens! This is the cheapest camp I've ever heard of!"

Abby turned to see her mom studying the white paper.

"This camp costs less than Ryan's camp—and his isn't a sleep-away camp!"

"I wanna go to Abby's camp, too!" said Ryan, sounding exactly like an eight-year-old.

"But you're already signed up for Camp Makonoweea," said his mom.

Mrs. Carnelia almost slipped and called it Camp Economeea, which is what she and her husband called it as a joke. (It was not a very fancy camp.)

"Ryan, you'll have a great time at your own camp," said Abby. "All your friends are going! Besides, I'll call you every once in a while."

"No, I don't think you'll be doing that," said her mother, reading one of the documents. "They have a no–cell phones rule. But they do have e-mail, so you can write to us."

Abby blinked at her. "No cell phones?"

Her mother shrugged. "I guess they want you to focus on the natural setting, the meaningful friendships, all that sort of thing."

Ryan was suddenly a lot happier.

Abby's parents had given her a sweet, shiny, metallic-purple cell phone as an early graduation gift, and Ryan had gone nuts with jealousy. He'd wanted one ever since. He was thrilled to see the look on Abby's face when she learned she'd have to do without hers. It definitely took the sting out of her being allowed to go to sleep-away camp.

"No cell phones! Oh yeah! Uh-huh! Can you feel it?" he sang. He danced around Abby, poking at her with his index fingers.

"Well, I guess I can look at the bright side," Abby responded, glaring at him.

"What's that, honey?" asked her mom.

"No little brothers."

CHAPTER
5
Ben

IN EASTPORT, the beginning of summer is a great time to be a sixth grader. It's not only the end of the school year, it's also the end of all your years at elementary school. The weather is gorgeous, you can walk or ride your bike every-where, and nobody can concentrate on anything serious. Not even the teachers.

For Abby, June meant a parade of special end-of-the-year days. There was Teacher Appreciation Day, the performance of the school musical, and Bad Hair Day (don't ask). There was even a tiny graduation ceremony for the sixth graders called Moving Up Day, to celebrate the move to middle school.

Before she even knew what hit her, she and her family

were piling into the minivan and starting the long drive to Camp Cadabra.

Abby never could read on long car rides; it gave her a headache. And her dad hadn't been able to find the power adapter for the DVD player. So Abby spent the drive to Camp Cadabra working on her knitting project: a rainbow-colored ski hat. It did seem a little bizarre to be making a big thick cozy warm hat on a blazing hot day in late June, but it helped to kill the time.

It also helped her focus on something other than her excitement and fear. Going to camp for the first time had had its high points, like shopping for all the stuff she was going to need. Clothes. Pillow. New bathing suit. Books to read. A little case for holding magic props, even though she didn't really have much yet.

But at the same time, Abby had no idea what she was getting herself into. All of it was new: sleep-away camp, not knowing anybody, and entering the realm of magic.

Still, she was grateful that the whole family had driven up to New Hampshire to drop her off—even her dad, who had just returned from twenty days of flying for his airline and was looking forward to two weeks at home.

Abby and Ryan were halfway through a game of Window Alphabet—you race to be the first person to find things outside of the car that start with the letters A to Z, in order—when the tires started making a crunching sound. Mr. Carnelia had just turned off of the main road.

"Now that's what I call a proper summer-camp driveway," he announced. They were on a long, crunchy gravel lane with towering pine trees on both sides.

Abby looked out the window just in time to see a new-looking, modern sign nailed to one of the pine trees: "Have a *magical* day at CAMP CADABRA!"

"S! S for 'sign,'" said Ryan.

"We're here, Ry," said Abby. "Game's over."

Mr. Carnelia rolled down his window. "And that's what I call proper summer-camp smell," he boomed.

Sure enough, New Hampshire smelled nothing like Connecticut. It was piney, and sunny, and foresty.

"I'm hot," announced Ryan.

"That's sort of the point of summer camp, isn't it?" asked Mr. Carnelia, running his hand over his bald spot. "Roughing it. The great outdoors. Eating mystery meat. Drinking bug juice. Short-sheeting a few beds."

Abby was just about to ask what short-sheeting was when the driveway ended. Suddenly, she was looking out the window at a huge, dusty, sunny parking lot, filled with families unloading cars. It looked like a minivan convention.

Camp counselors in bright red T-shirts walked among

the cars, clutching clipboards and directing traffic. Everyone was milling around, unloading, asking questions, hugging parents, taking pictures, and aiming camcorders.

Mr. Carnelia parked the car, opened the door, and stepped out. "Well, I'll be hornswoggled," he intoned. "So this is where they grow young magicians."

The rest of the Carnelias got out of the car and looked around, blinking in the bright noon sunshine.

"I'll go see if I can find somebody in charge," said Abby's mom. She headed off in the general direction of the buildings, whose roofs peeked out from the pine trees nearby.

Mr. Carnelia began unloading stuff from the trunk and carrying it over to a line of low tables marked LUGGAGE. Ryan ran over to a nearby minivan, where a boy was doing magic tricks for a couple of other kids.

Abby was just standing there, taking it all in, when she heard a voice coming from her right.

"Excuse me—do you know if there's lunch?"

It was a tall, easy-moving boy, maybe fourteen, with freckles, hazel eyes, floppy brown hair.

Abby turned to him. "What?"

He held up the packet of papers in his hand. "The welcome stuff doesn't say anything about lunch. You don't know if there's first-day lunch, do you?"

Abby shook her head. "No, I don't know. We—we just got here about a minute ago."

"Oh, okay. No biggie." He glanced around the parking area as though he was considering whether to leave, but then he seemed to change his mind.

"I'm Ben. Close-up or illusionary?"

"Hi, I'm—I'm Abby. What did you say?"

"Close-up or illusionary?"

It was ancient Greek to her.

"Oh, I—I'm really new to all this," she managed.

Ben was persistent. "No, I mean, what are you into? Close-up tricks or stage illusions?"

"Oh, right," she said. She thought briefly about her trick—her one real trick. "Close-up, I guess."

"Hey, really?" said Ben. "That's awesome. Me, too. Check this out!"

He pulled a car key out of his jeans pocket and put it on his open palm.

"And now . . . this is the crazy part. I'm not going to touch this key. I'm not going to blow on it. No strings attached. It's nothing more than . . . a momentary flux of gravity."

He squeezed one eye shut—and that's when it happened. The key, lying flat on his palm, slowly rose up on its edge and flopped over.

That's all it did. But it happened so slowly, so clearly, and so close to Abby's face, that she felt a shockwave of amazement.

Ben noticed her look and beamed happily. "I love close-up," he said.

"That's a *really* good trick," she said, because it was. "Will you tell me how you did it?"

She knew that magicians weren't supposed to reveal their secrets to their audience, but she didn't know if magicians couldn't tell *other magicians*. Maybe that kind of thing didn't apply in an all-magician camp.

"Well, this is going to sound weird," Ben said quietly, almost whispering, "but I *don't know*. It's just something that I seem to be able to do. I noticed one day that if I just squint one eye—"

And he did it again. He squinted one eye, and the key rolled up and over on his hand.

Abby's stomach practically dropped out of her body. For a moment, she was struck speechless, motionless, and brainless. Could this be happening? Had she just met another person with some tiny magical power and no way to explain it? Maybe she wasn't the only one!

This changed everything. This was *huge*. Ten minutes at summer camp and her sense of freakiness and isolation was starting to crumble.

"*Are you kidding?*" she gushed. She grabbed his forearm, not even noticing his surprise. "You really don't know how you do it? Oh my gosh, I have to tell you something. I'm just like you! A few weeks ago, I was chopping eggs—well, never mind about that. See, I have a trick, too. Not a trick, really; the thing is—"

"Witches 3," Mrs. Carnelia announced, appearing from nowhere, with a red-shirted camp counselor following just behind. She had chosen that exact moment to return. "Isn't that cute? The boys' cabins are all called Wizards, and the girls' are all Witches."

Abby was suddenly hot and frustrated. "Mom, just a second, okay? I'm kind of in the middle of something here."

"Well, introduce us, honey!" Mrs. Carnelia nudged Abby's shoulder.

For a second, Abby couldn't remember his name. He rescued her.

"I'm Ben Wheeler," he said, offering his hand to Abby's parents in what Abby was sure they'd think was a very mature way.

"Hello, Ben," said Mr. Carnelia. "We're Abby's parents." He glanced around. "There's supposed to be a brother, too."

"Wheeler, Wheeler," muttered the counselor, checking her clipboard. "Here we go—Wheeler, Benjamin. You're in Wizards 4. You're gonna be with Tony—he's your

counselor. You'll love him; he's great. Want me to introduce you?"

Abby's brain answered for Ben: *No no no no! I mean, no,
thank you. I'm going to hang out here with my new friend Abby. I've just
discovered that we have the most astonishing thing in common—*

But Ben's brain had other plans. "Sure," he said, shrug-
ging.

The counselor wagged a finger toward the Carnelias.
"You guys are all set?"

Mr. Carnelia nodded. "Witches 3, up the hill past the
dining hall. We'll find it. Thanks."

"Okeydoke. Come on, Ben, I'll take you to meet Tony,
and then I'll show you where lunch is set up."

Ben perked up. "Lunch?" he said. "There's lunch?"

Ben and the counselor walked away.

Mr. and Mrs. Carnelia set about rounding up Ryan and
getting Abby signed in. If they saw any of the excitement
and confusion on Abby's face, they didn't say so.

CHAPTER
6
Camp

"LEMME HEAR YOU SAY *YEAH*, Witchezzz!" said Claudia.

She was the red-shirted, college-age, slightly pudgy, completely pumped-up counselor in front of Abby's cabin. Every time she shouted, her side-mounted ponytail flounced like a pom-pom.

"*Yeah!*" shouted Abby and the other girls.

"Lemme hear you say *Rock*, Witchezzzz!" said the counselor, louder now.

"*Rock!*" shouted the girls, louder still.

"All right, now, gimme the W!" She thrust her hand into the middle of the circle of girls, with her three middle fingers sticking up like a letter "W," and they all knocked fists in midair. It was a corny way to build cabin togetherness and spirit, Abby knew, but she had to admit that it was working. She was already feeling some sisterly affection for the five other girl magicians in her cabin.

"All riiiiiight!" shouted Claudia, pumping her fist in the air by itself now. "Listen up, Witches. I'm gonna be straight with you: there are at least three times as many boys as girls at this camp. But this is day one, Witches. And by day fourteen, you know what we're going to show the world? That girls make just as good magicians as boys. Or *better*, right?"

"*Right!*" shouted the girls, definitely pumped up now.

"All right, so listen up, ladies. You are in Witches 3. It's the coolest, classiest cabin in Camp Cadabra. Oh, sure, it may look just like the other girls' cabins. It may be on the same hill as the other girls' cabins. It may have the same *view* as the other girls' cabins. But it's not the same. This one is *special*. You know why, Witches?"

The girls shook their heads, grinning.

"Because only Witches 3 has Claudia. That's me. And only Witches 3 has the six of you. And as you shall see, *that* is what makes this cabin the coolest and the classiest. Now let's get inside so I can show you around."

Fired up with excitement, the girls pushed their way into the cabin.

Now, a word about the Camp Cadabra cabins. When you

read the word *cabin*, you're probably thinking of, say, a *log* cabin, or a *camp* cabin, or a cabin in the woods. Something simple, and bare bones, and woodsy.

But the cabins at Camp Cadabra were quite another story.

This camp, Abby soon discovered, was not all about "roughing it." Abby had never seen any other sleep-away summer camps, but she could tell right away that on the comfort scale, this one was Extra Cushy.

It was brand new, for one thing. Absolutely spotless. It even had that fresh-cut lumber smell that seemed to say, "You're the first people who ever slept here."

The cabin was air-conditioned, too. The cots weren't cots—they were like hotel beds, deep and comfortable. When you lay down, you felt like you were sinking down halfway to China.

Each cabin had both indoor and outdoor showers, complete with marble tile floors, and a fridge for late-night snacks. There was even a laptop on a desk in the corner, always connected to the Internet—"so you can write to your folks and tell them what a blast you're having," as Claudia put it.

It's a good thing Dad didn't stay long enough to really see this place, Abby thought. *He'd have hated all the luxury.*

"Tell you what, Witches," Claudia was saying after the girls had picked out their beds and stashed their suitcases and duffel bags. "Why don't we go around and introduce ourselves? Tell me your name, what grade you're going into, where you're from, and what makes you magic."

Abby felt a little shiver when she heard that phrase.

One by one, the girls gave their introductions. There was an Allison, a Debbie, a Becky, two Sarahs (actually, one Sarah and one Sara, with no "h") and, of course, Abby. They were all going into sixth or seventh grade.

Abby began to worry, though, when she heard their magic backgrounds.

"I've been doing magic since I was six," said Debbie.

"I do magic shows at my street's block party every summer," said Becky.

"I won second place in our school's talent show. I did the Professor's Nightmare," said one of the Sarahs.

"And how about you, Abby?" asked Claudia, her sidesaddle ponytail flouncing.

Abby smiled nervously and looked around the room. What was she supposed to say? *Um, I can make an egg spin by itself, but otherwise, I've never done a single trick in my life? And by the way, it has to be hard-boiled, and I have to be pulling on my ears?*

"Um," she began. "Actually, I'm really just—just kind of a beginner. I want to learn more about magic, and I figured this would be the place." She managed a weak smile.

44

"Excellent," said Claudia, beaming. She reached over to give Abby a supportive shoulder squeeze. "This really *is* the place."

Abby was not so sure.

No-H Sara was a tiny little person, skinny and short—even her blond hair was sort of fuzzy and lightweight. Abby half worried that if the wind ever picked up, No-H Sara would have to be weighted down so she wouldn't blow away.

But as far as Abby was concerned, there were two great things about No-H Sara. First, she was a cheery little chatterbox—and since she felt like she was about a thousand miles from home, that kind of perkiness was just what Abby needed.

Second, without any discussion, No-H Sara had simply adopted Abby. This was Camp Cadabra's very first summer of operation, but No-H Sara acted as though she owned the place.

"Did you notice anything about the buildings?" No-H Sara was saying. She and Abby meandered toward the cafeteria building in the last half hour before dinner. The beautifully groomed path dipped in and out of the woods, which offered cooler air than the grassy hillside itself.

Abby shook her head.

45

Sara spread her hands wide. "The Dumbledore build-ing? Hermione Cafeteria? Wormtail Game Room? Hello?"

"Ahhhhh," Abby said, smiling as she picked up a pine-cone to study it as they walked. "Harry Potter. Everything's named after Harry Potter?"

"Exactly. I mean, we're not exactly walking around with robes and memorizing spells and flying on brooms and stuff. Although that would be kinda cool."

Abby nodded. "It makes the buildings easy to remem-ber, though."

"The thing is, if you ask me, this place is really only half a magic camp," No-H Sara continued. "I mean, in the morn-ing, yeah, we have our three magic classes. But after lunch, it's just like a regular summer camp with regular activities. Look at this stuff!"

She held up the shiny, colorful pages of the "red book"— the camper handbook that Claudia had given them. "Tennis, archery, soccer, arts and crafts, horseback riding. Or water-front. If you sign up for waterfront, you get to do sailing, water-skiing, or parasailing. I love parasailing."

Abby peered over at the photos. "What's parasailing?"

"Oh, you know," said Sara matter-of-factly. "Where they hook you up to a big giant kite on a rope, and then they pull you along with a motorboat so you fly way up in the air."

Abby was amazed. "And you've *done* that before?"

"Oh yeah." Sara cocked her head as she nodded. "I'm from Florida."

Abby raised her eyebrows, impressed. "And have you done *this* before?"

"What?"

"Magic camp? Summer camp?"

"Well, nobody's done *this* camp. They just opened up," said No-H Sara the Tour Guide. "But I've been going to summer camps, like, forever. My parents believe in exposing us to the world."

Sara stepped up onto a gleaming wooden bench, walked along its length like a tightrope walker, then hopped down at the far end to join Abby. "So what are you gonna sign up for? I'm gonna do Stage Magic. You wanna do it with me?"

Already, Abby had heard plenty about Stage Magic. It was the most popular morning class by far, because that's where you got to work with the big flashy illusions, like making people float in the air or chopping them into thirds.

And it's easy to understand why those classes were so popular. After all, when you're at home, you hardly ever get to try that kind of magic, since you need a lot of big, expensive, special equipment to do it. "All the world's a stage," Shakespeare once wrote, but he forgot the part about how hard it is to fit those six-foot cabinets into the back of your parents' Toyota Camry.

Abby couldn't help smiling at the thought of tiny Sara, the human hummingbird, flittering about the stage among the gigantic Cabinets of Mystery.

But Abby had no interest in striding across the stage, gesturing grandly at assistants wearing sparkly leotards. In fact, although she didn't dare let anybody at Cadabra know it, she didn't have much interest in performing *at all*. She just wanted to discover the secrets of her magical power.

"I—I haven't decided yet," Abby replied.

She *had* flipped through the red book, looking over all the available classes. Yet amazingly enough, Abby hadn't found anything called "Earlobe Power: The Rotational Characteristics of Poultry Products."

Instead, she planned to sign up for what looked like the next best things. "I was thinking of maybe Card Magic, Coin Manipulation, and Dinner Table Magic," she said.

"Huh!" said Sara. *Swing!* Sara had picked up a stick and was swatting at branches like they were baseballs. "So you're into the close-up magic, then." *Swing!*

"Well, if you're so into close-up, then why don't you sign up for Impromptu? That's the best kind of close-up anyway, I think. You know, it's all, like, spur-of-the-moment stuff, where you don't have to set up the trick beforehand."

My egg thing certainly seems to fit that category, thought Abby. "Sure! I'll try that one! Unless, I mean—"

"Unless what?"

Abby took a breath. "Well, let me ask you. Do you think they might have any kind of classes where you can learn about, like . . . *real* magic?"

No-H Sara stopped on the path and rested the bat-stick on her shoulder. She looked at Abby with a cocked eyebrow.

"What do you mean, *real* magic?"

"You know, like—weird stuff you can't explain. I saw a newspaper ad that talked about, you know, unexplained phenomena. Like moving stuff with your mind and stuff. What should I sign up for if I'm interested in that kind of magic?"

No-H Sara studied Abby for what seemed like a very long time.

"What you should sign up for is *Crazy Class*," she said finally. "Only nut cases believe in stuff like that. My grandma always says, 'The only people who believe in the invisible are people with nothing visible to believe in.'"

Sara pounded her bat-stick on the freshly paved pathway. "Now come on. They're gonna open the doors for dinner in like six seconds, and I don't want to have to sit at the losers' table!" She turned and trotted ahead.

Maybe that's where I belong, thought Abby miserably. *At the losers' table.*

She picked up the pace and followed her new friend out of the woods.

CHAPTER
7
Class

"C'MON, ABBY! TRY IT AGAIN. You'll get it."

No-H Sara and Abby sat side by side at the long, pine tables in the Snape building, practicing what they'd learned the first day in Coin Manipulation class.

"I don't know, Sara. It looks so easy when *you* do it, but I . . ." She picked up her quarter and tried the Thumb Palm again—and messed it up again.

She looked around at the fifteen other kids in the class. The Snape building wasn't really a building; it was actually more of an open-air pavilion. It had a roof and a floor, but no walls, so it kept some of that breezy, summer camp atmosphere.

The counselor in charge, who identified himself as

Chaz, was a complete and total magic nerd. He knew the name and history of every coin move, said he owned over 200 magic DVDs, and insisted that his dad had once met David Copperfield's lawyer. He was also blindingly good at coin tricks; it was pretty clear to Abby how Chaz had spent his free time growing up.

Abby, however, was having trouble with the coin stuff.

"Is it all sleight of hand?" she asked Sara as her quarter clanked to the table yet again. "I'm gonna have to spend the rest of my summer in front of the camcorder practicing!"

(Abby had learned that all decent magicians nowadays do their practicing in front of a camcorder. "Nobody practices in front of a mirror anymore," No-H Sara had said matter-of-factly. "If you're looking at yourself in the mirror, you can't be looking at your hands or your trick. So you can't use misdirection with your eyes. Get it?")

The only thing that made Coin Manipulation bearable was hanging out with Sara.

"Listen, tell you what," she was saying. "Forget the Thumb Palm—you're never gonna need that anyway. I know some really easy ones that look a lot better anyway. Check this out."

She showed Abby how to flip a coin, catch it in midair, and figure out whether it was heads or tails before she even looked at it. "Right before you slap it down, you feel it with your thumb, see?" she said. "Really fast. The back of the quarter is all rough; the front, the heads side, has a big smooth president on it. So you can tell which way it's facing."

Abby felt a flood of gratitude for Sara's kindness. Overall, though, she was getting discouraged. This whole operation seemed to be all about tricks. A trick was not real magic. It was something that was supposed to look like magic, but actually stayed 100 percent within the laws of physics.

Chaz said he knew a great way to make a coin disappear, for example, but what he really meant was he knew a great way to hide it so the audience thought it had disappeared. In Abby's next class, Cards, the counselor said she'd show the kids how to make a card rise from the deck, but actually she showed them how to push the card up in a way the audience couldn't see.

Abby wasn't having a terrible time. She was making friends, and she was inspired to see how seriously all the other kids were taking this hobby. She even picked out a couple of favorite tricks and decided she'd work on them until they looked smooth and polished.

But deep down, the first couple of classes left Abby with a nagging worry about the sort of magic that she was learning at Camp Cadabra: It was all fake. All of it.

And then she went to Impromptu.

The class was held indoors, in a big, bright room in the

Hagrid building. It looked a little like the science classrooms she'd seen during a tour of the Eastport Middle School, with long tables topped by thick black stone. As she walked in, two counselors were setting up what looked like place settings for dinner—plates, silverware, glasses, napkins—at each seat.

As she walked in, she saw someone she knew.

"Ben!" she said happily, waving to him.

Ben brushed the floppy hair from his eyes and smiled.

"Hey," he said. "Abby, right?"

"Right," she said.

He adjusted his knife and fork absentmindedly. "So how's your first real day of camp going?"

"Good," she said. "Fun stuff." She took a breath and pointed to the chair next to him. "Can I sit here?"

"I'm sorry, ma'am, we're expecting a party of sixteen at any moment." He grinned at her.

"Well, they'll just have to wait, won't they?" she said, flouncing down onto the seat. Her day, and her mood, were rapidly improving.

This, Abby thought, is the perfect opportunity to ask Ben about his magical power. She just didn't know how to bring it up.

As it turned out, there wasn't time.

"Good morning, my people!" came a voice from the front of the room.

Abby turned to look. It was a short, pudgy guy wearing a flowered Hawaiian shirt and a greasy, blond ponytail.

"My name is Ferd. Kindly note that it's not Fred—it's Ferd. Short for Ferdinand. Please make a note of it. And for the next two weeks, I'll be teaching you amateurs about the marvels of impromptu magic."

He was strolling slowly down the aisles between the tables, like a king surveying his peasants, but his voice was high and thin.

"Impromptu. Adjective: 'without prior planning.' In magic, there's nothing better. You're hanging out with friends. Or waiting for the waiter. Or waiting to be picked up from school. Or you're at someone else's house, and the six-year-old says, 'Do a trick!' What are you going to do—run home to get your suitcase full of props?"

Ferd opened his eyes wide, expectantly.

"I think not!"

Abby, highly entertained, snuck a look at Ben's face. He was fascinated, too, with a you-gotta-be-kidding-me expression.

"In such scenarios," Ferd continued, "impromptu magic is your only way out. You pick up something that you've got on hand, be it a salt shaker, be it a dollar bill, be it a writing implement. And you commence to conjure."

With this, Ferd stopped by one of the tables, picked up

a salt shaker, and wrapped it in a napkin. Then he picked up a pepper shaker—"the spice of life!" he declared—and sprinkled some pepper onto the napkin.

Then he crushed the napkin. The salt shaker inside was gone.

"Now, *impromptu* may mean 'no preparation.' But what is unprepared, my people, are the *props*—not the *magician*. You, my people, must do quite a lot of preparation—and you're going to be doing it here, in my class, over the next two weeks. You are my Frankensteins. I am going to create you. I am going to turn you into impromptu magicians, capable of performing miracles with ordinary unprepared objects—on an audience, I assure you, that is completely unprepared for *you*."

Ferd had returned to the front of the room, where he picked up a spoon from his place setting.

"Today, we talk about presentation. In today's class, you will not learn a trick, you will not perform any tricks, you will not even discuss tricks. We will learn the art of *presentation*. Showmanship. Patter. Personal style. If you master the presentation, the trick part will come easily. As Harry Houdini didn't say, the secret is only the last five percent. All right: kindly examine your spoon."

The campers, intrigued by Ferd and *his* memorable presentation style, picked up their spoons and held them up off the table, following his lead.

"For the sake of argument, my people, let us say that our objective here is to make this spoon levitate—to make it float in the air. What I want you to do is to make up a half-decent *trigger*."

He thrust out his arm, pointing around the room as though he were trying to pick out the murderer in a crowd of suspects.

"Consider, if you will, the best magic trick you've ever seen. I don't care if it was on a stage, on a table in front of you, or in a movie. Whatever it was, it had a trigger: something that the magician did to make the magic happen, something that showed how *he* was in control."

He waggled his fingers mysteriously at the spoon.

"If you're a six-year-old," he went on, "the trigger is saying, 'hocus pocus.' If you're ten and not very imaginative, maybe you wave your hands. If you're a mind reader, you close your eyes and frown. If you're *Bewitched*, you wiggle your nose. If you're Harry Potter, you point your wand and say something in fake Latin. These would be your *triggers*."

He demonstrated a few triggers, waving, staring, pointing, waggling his fingers.

"The trigger is only for show," he went on, "but it's an important part of the illusion. So I want you to take four minutes to consider the trigger. I want to see your trigger. Surprise me. Be different. Cultivate your own style. Make it fit your personality. Okay, go."

57

The room burst into murmurs and giggles as the campers turned their attention to triggers. Ben held out his spoon and glared at it, eyebrows high. Abby laughed and responded with a trigger of her own: holding the spoon over her head and blowing on it. Ferd stalked the room, muttering comments like "Fine, fine" and "A bit tired, wouldn't you say?"

Eventually, Ferd moved on to the finer points of magic presentation—things like patter (what you say while you're doing the trick), misdirection (making the audience look where you want them to look), and conclusion (wrapping up the trick in a satisfying way).

Impromptu was nearly over when Abby had a startling thought. She had discovered her pointless power by accident, by tugging on her earlobes looking for an earring. *That* was the trigger—a *real* trigger.

For weeks now, she'd been wondering how long she'd had her magical power. Did she just develop it now, at age eleven? Had she had it for weeks?

Suddenly, though, she had a crazy realization.

I'll bet I've always had the power, she thought. *But that was the first time in my life I ever did that trigger when there was an egg on the counter in front of me. If I hadn't pulled my earlobes at that moment, I might never have discovered my power at all!*

Abby wasn't quite sure whether that would have been a good thing or not.

"Abby?"

It was Ben, looking at her with concern.

"Earth to Abby."

She straightened up. "Sorry, what'd you say?"

"I said, do you wanna sit with me at lunch? They're serving a special today—mystery meat."

"My favorite," she said. "Let's go."

This, she hoped, would be more than just a lunch with a fellow camper. It would be her first chance to compare notes with another person who had real magic.

CHAPTER 8
Lunch

L IKE EVERYTHING ELSE AT CAMP CADABRA, the dining hall wasn't anything like what you'd expect to find at a summer camp; it was magnificent. Inside, it was like a grand Swiss castle, with a huge, soaring cathedral ceiling and gigantic windows overlooking the lake.

Oh—and I should probably mention the food.

This was not camp food. This was not Jell-O cubes, fruit cocktail, and defrosted trays of fried nuggets. This was a salad bar twenty feet long, a taco bar every other day, and a pasta station at every meal, where you could pick the kind of noodles you liked and what kind of sauce you wanted on it. At breakfast, there were two little guys who would make omelets or pancakes with whatever stuff you wanted in them, like bacon and cheese for the omelets, chocolate chips or blueberries for the pancakes.

Where on earth did this camp get its money? Abby couldn't help but remember what her mom had said when she'd opened the brochures: not how *expensive* this camp was going to be, but that the price seemed so low. Abby imagined that some famous magician, some guy who'd gotten his start at a magic camp at age eleven, had donated some of his millions to build a new one. Or something.

As Abby set her tray down next to Ben and stepped over the padded leather bench to sit down, he was chatting with a buddy from his cabin across the table. She waited for a break in the conversation, took a big gulp of her lemonade, and then dove in.

"So. Ben."

He turned his head. "So. Abby."

"Um. Listen, I really need to talk to you for a sec."

He looked away, as though the tacos on his plate had gotten *really* interesting.

Oh, great, Abby thought. *I've known the guy for, what, six minutes? He probably thinks I'm a stalker.*

"Okay, I'm really sorry if this is gonna sound weird and strange. Will you promise not to be creeped out?"

61

"I can't really promise," Ben said after a moment. "But I will say that it takes a *lot* to creep me out. My dad's let me watch horror movies since I was six."

Abby smiled, only slightly less nervous. She took a breath. "Okay. Remember when you showed me your key trick yesterday in the parking lot?"

Ben nodded.

"And I asked you how you did it, and you said you didn't really know. You *said* that, right? You said it just happens when you squint one eye, or whatever."

"Well, yeah. I mean, I tell everybody that."

"You do?" she said. "You're completely open about it? I can't believe it! Because, listen, I have a trick like that, too."

And there it was. She was spilling it. She started talking faster. "Not a trick—a *power*. Just like yours! Except with an egg, not a key. And I don't have any idea how I do it, either! And I've been thinking that I'm some kind of freak or something. I thought I was the only one in the world with a power I can't explain. And that's the whole reason I signed up for this camp! Because I thought maybe I could learn more about it, or master it, or develop it, or something like that. But everybody's just doing *trick* tricks, like magic tricks—and that's all great and everything, but it's nothing like what you and I do! And so yesterday, when I saw you do that, I was just so happy, SO happy, because it was like, hey, I just can't believe that there's someone else who's got anything like my—"

She got stuck there. She didn't know whether to say "power" or "problem."

"—well, anyway, there's somebody else like me! And I'm just so happy to meet you, and I want to know everything you know about your power."

Ben was no longer smiling. In fact, he looked a little uncomfortable. If you'd seen his face, you would have thought that he'd just been attacked by a crazy person.

"Yeah. Well—well, okay," he said, frowning. "Look, Abby. I mean, I love magic. I've been doing it since I got my first magic kit in kindergarten. I've won a couple of awards. I do close-up at a restaurant every Sunday night, going table to table. But I—I'm not gonna sit here and tell you I have magic *powers*."

Abby could almost hear the next thing he wanted to say: *I'm not totally insane, like you are.*

"But your key trick!" she said. "You said you don't know how you do it, right?"

"Of *course* I know how I do it! I practiced for about three months to get it that good!"

Abby was thunderstruck. "But you said—you said—I mean, I asked you how you did it, and you said you didn't know! You said it flipped over whenever you did that squinting thing!"

Ben shook his head. "That's just patter, Abby! Whenever anybody says, 'How do you do it?' that's just what I say! If you tell 'em how you really do it, you destroy the trick. You ruin it for them, because everybody *wants* to believe that magic is real. But if you tell 'em even *you* don't know how it works, you keep the mystery alive. You keep it going. It makes the trick even better! It's just patter, Abby."

Abby felt tears welling up in her eyes. She was suddenly roasting hot. How could she have been such an idiot?

She stood up and turned away, walking fast across the dining hall. *Of course he doesn't have a power, you moron!* she told herself. *It's only you, and it's always been only you, and you just made yourself look like a first-class idiot!*

It wasn't until Abby reached the salad bar, stretched out across one end of the building like a chrome-and-glass battleship, that the world stopped spinning long enough for her to stop and compose herself. Now she was special, all right—a laughingstock. She was the one kid at Camp Cadabra who was loopy enough to think that she *really* was magic.

She stood there, leaning against the glass sneeze guard over the fancy lettuce bin. How would she explain to her parents why she wanted to leave camp after only one day?

"Abby." Someone was tapping her shoulder.

It was Ben.

"Abby. What just happened back there?"

She looked up at the dark wooden beams of the high cafeteria ceiling, trying to stop herself from crying. She said nothing.

"Listen," he said. "The thing you said about an egg. Is that true? Is that for real?"

She gave a tiny nod, still looking away.

There was a pause, and then Ben went on.

"I mean, look, I'll be honest with you. I've never seen a trick that I couldn't figure out, or at least that I couldn't think of a way to do it. But, I mean . . ." He stopped and sighed. "I mean—could you show me?"

Abby wiped at her eye and sneaked a look at him for the first time. "What?"

Ben studied her face seriously. "I want to see your egg thing. Would you show me?"

When she hesitated, Ben took charge. He scanned the salad bar and quickly found what he was looking for: a basket of hard-boiled eggs. He grabbed one and pressed it into Abby's hand.

"Show me. I want to see it."

It took her a minute to make up her mind. But Abby realized that, at this point, she had nothing to lose. She knew she couldn't make herself look any sillier.

"Hold out your hand," she told him.

She grabbed his hand from underneath to steady it. She put the egg on his hand. She let go.

"All right," she said. "This is my power."

She tugged on her earlobes. "This is my trigger," she said, with a hint of a smile.

The egg began to turn on Ben's palm.

What Abby learned that day is that magicians and normal people react to magic tricks very differently. A big, flashy trick that blows away normal people may not excite a magician very much, because a magician can guess how it's done.

What really impresses a magician is a trick that *can't* be figured out, no matter how small. And Ben knew that was what he was seeing. There was no breeze, no wires, no magnets, no little tiny trained hamsters. It was an egg that *he* had picked out of the basket, on *his* palm—and Abby was three feet away.

It was *impossible*.

She finally took her eyes off the egg to look at Ben. His mind had been blown to smithereens. He simply couldn't process what he was seeing.

He didn't say anything for a long time.

He looked at the egg very closely, holding it right up to his eye. Then he looked at Abby, his eyes intense under his floppy bangs. "Abby," he said. "Either I've just seen the greatest magic trick ever invented . . ." He swallowed. "Or you really are a witch."

CHAPTER 9
Show

IF YOU ASKED HER NOW, Abby could still tell you every single detail of that first day of magic camp. Her emotions were on a roller coaster all day. And in those moments by the salad bar, she went from feeling like the loneliest person on earth to knowing that she had a close friend she could trust.

She remembers playing soccer in the afternoon. All that running around, full out, was just what she needed. By the end of the game, she was exhausted and exhilarated. And hungry. After a quick rinse in the outdoor shower at Witches 3, she headed with her cabin mates over to the dining hall for dinner.

She didn't wind up sitting with them, however. While

she was standing at the pasta bar, ladling pesto sauce onto her angel hair noodles, Ben came directly over to her. He didn't waste any time telling her what was on his mind.

"I know what you have to do, Abby."

She put the ladle back in the saucepot and glanced at him. "Oh, hello to you, too, Ben. I'm fine—thanks for asking."

Either he didn't get it, or he didn't hear it.

"I've been thinking all afternoon. I know what you have to do. You have to do your egg trick at Camper Show."

Camper Show was the highlight of each day at Camp Cadabra. After dinner each night, everybody piled into the brand-new, high-tech, outdoor theater, and Camp Cadabra turned into a breathtaking magic festival. First, at 7:00 p.m., the campers watched what they called Magic Show—a performance by a professional magician who'd been flown in for the evening from Las Vegas or New York or wherever.

Then, at 7:30, there was Camper Show; that's when a few fellow campers got the chance to try out the tricks they'd been working on in front of a live audience.

Abby picked up her tray and turned toward her table. "Camper Show? Thank you. I'm flattered. But seriously— are you crazy?"

"Come on, Abby! Why not?"

"They'll laugh me off the stage, Ben! It's not a good trick. It's not *even* a trick. It's small, it's short, it's boring, it doesn't go anywhere, and it's pointless. It's *lame!*"

Three hundred kids all laughing at her—now *that* would be the perfect wrap-up to her wobbly Camp Cadabra experience.

Ben nodded, slurping his milkshake. "Okay, fine. So we'll goose it up."

She cocked an eyebrow. "Goose it up?"

"I'll admit, it's a little small for a stage show. So we'll make it play bigger."

"Like how? How do you make it big enough to see from the back of the room? Use a dinosaur egg?"

He grinned. "Why? Can you spin those too?"

"I don't know," Abby said. "Go get me one from the salad bar, and I'll give it a shot."

Ben pretended that he was about to get up from the bench to go get one. But then he stopped short and sat down again. "Seriously, Abby. I think you should perform it. You have nothing to lose and a lot to gain."

"Like what?"

"Well, at the very least, you'll meet a lot of people. You'll get fantastic experience in appearing before a big crowd. And if your trick really is . . . you know, more than just a trick . . ."

He trailed off for a moment. His face told Abby all she needed to know: that he was still having trouble getting used to the fact that she had an actual power, that he wasn't sure he should believe it. *That's okay,* she thought. *I'm still not sure I should believe it myself.*

"You mean, if I'm not making this up about my power," she prodded him.

He looked down, but he nodded. "Right. If it's for real—if it's for real, then at least you'll be showing the entire camp at once. And if anybody here knows anything about it—you know, about sort of—unexplainable powers—then you'll hear about it."

Abby considered this point as she twirled the pasta on her fork. If her little stunt could impress the other magicians as much as it had impressed Ben, then maybe it wouldn't be so bad. And it would be a great opportunity for the camp's counselors to see it—real magicians. Maybe one of them might know, at last, something about unexplained phenomena.

She closed her eyes for a brief moment, and then shook her head. "It's just too small, Ben," she said finally.

"Well, if that's what you're worried about, don't. Plenty of kids are planning to do close-up tricks in Camper Show—little tiny tricks with dice, or cards, or coins. That's why they have a cameraman!"

"They what?"

"There's a guy with a video camera, and the trick is projected on big screens on either side of the stage," he said. "Everybody can see it. You don't have to worry."

"But it's just not any good as a trick. After all these people get up there with mind-reading and card routines and sawing people in half, I can't just get up there, spin an egg, and walk off."

"I know," Ben replied. "But I've been working on this part, and I think I know how to make it work. Look, Camper Show isn't some birthday party or some talent show. You're not performing for normal people; you're performing to an audience of magicians. Magicians have a different amazement threshold. We've got to play up the impossibility of it. Your trick isn't especially dazzling, but it does violate the laws of physics, and we have to make sure the kids know that."

"Okay, how?" she asked.

His leg was bouncing up and down, something it seemed to do by itself when Ben's mind was racing. "We're gonna need a dozen spools of thread. A couple of Nerf balls. And a ruler, and a terrarium from the Nature Station."

She had no idea what he was talking about. So she said, "I have no idea what you're talking about."

"And a dozen hard-boiled eggs."

She still didn't get it. "Why a dozen? Why do we need all that stuff?"

"I'll explain on the way. Finish up; we've got a scavenger hunt ahead of us."

The fourth night of Camp Cadabra's first two-seek session was cool and breezy, a welcome break from the heat of the first few days. The audience of campers and counselors wore sweaters and sweatshirts for that night's Camper Show.

There was no audition process for each evening's show. You signed up at lunch with a little description of your act. Truth is, the camp didn't really need auditions to ensure the quality of the show. The terror of looking like a bumbling idiot in front of three hundred fellow magicians was enough pressure to scare away the really lame acts. Usually, Camper Show included very good tricks presented by very talented campers.

Abby was quite sure that she would be the exception.

After dinner that night, it took No-H Sara ten minutes to persuade Abby to leave the Witches 3 cabin.

"Come on, girl!" Sara said, pounding the open doorway in frustration. "If we don't go right now, we're not gonna get good seats!"

Abby had been working with Ben on a presentation of the egg trick for two days, feverishly trying to come up with something that wouldn't seem too pathetic. She'd learned her patter, rehearsed the setup. She could practically do it in her sleep. And yet—

"I feel like I'm gonna throw up," Abby moaned, flopping back onto her bed. No-H Sara walked back into the cabin and kneeled down next to Abby.

"Abby, come on," she implored. "You said yourself you've got it down cold! It's going to be fine! We're all gonna be screaming for you. And besides, everyone's here to learn and get better, right? Everyone roots for everyone. What are you worried about?"

"Auuuugh!" Abby covered her face with her hands. What was she worried about? *Everything.* Nobody except Ben knew that, in fact, Abby had never done a single trick in front of an audience. The egg thing was all she could do. And the thought of three hundred kids seeing right through her was almost more than she could bear.

And that's if the trick worked. And if they could see it. And if they didn't think it was lame. And if she didn't freeze, faint, or puke—or all three at once.

Sara stepped forward and used the only remaining persuasion tactic she could think of: she started tickling Abby under the armpits.

"Okay—okay stop!" Abby cried out, shivering and giggling. She squirmed off of the bed, stood up, and backed away. "Okay, fine. I'm going. But if I pass out, you're calling 911."

"It's a deal," said Sara. "Now let's get going."

When they arrived at the Weasley Theater, Abby checked the bulletin board in the lobby. That's where the show committee posted, each night, the lineup of performers for that evening. Her name appeared as the fifth performer out of nine. That suited her fine; she didn't want to be either the first or the last magician in the show. That would be much more pressure than she could bear.

Abby took her seat in the front row of soft, reclining chairs, along with the other campers who'd be performing. As the lights went down, she caught a glimpse of Ben a few rows back. He gave her a double thumbs-up, but Abby wondered if he was as confident in her as he said he was.

The show opened with a ninth-grade camper performing his version of the Zombie. It's a standard stage illusion where, as music plays, a shiny silver sphere appears to float with a mind of its own, balancing delicately on the edge of a silk scarf before ducking behind the magician's back. The campers, who all knew how hard the Zombie is to perform properly, went wild.

Next came a card-manipulation trick involving two-handed fans of cards; alas, it went terribly wrong that night. The magician, a thirteen-year-old from Pennsylvania, was sweating too much in the stage lights and wound up dropping cards all over the stage.

That's going to be me right there, Abby told herself.

A tiny nine-year-old girl was up next, performing to music. It was an unusual routine, involving white-to-rainbow color changes, first of silk scarves, then paper flowers, then finally confetti. The crowd loved it.

While the fourth act went on—a mind-reading trick—Abby walked over to the stairs at the side of the stage, where a teenaged stage hand clipped a wireless microphone to Abby's blouse. "You're gonna do great," he said helpfully. "Knock 'em dead."

And then it was time.

Abby walked up the four stairs to the stage and somehow made it to the center.

"Hi guys," she said, her voice a little shaky. She wasn't used to hearing her voice amplified a hundred times, booming across the outdoor theater, under the stars.

The lights were shining directly into her eyes, making it almost impossible to see all those hundreds of people watching her, waiting for her to do something impressive. She took a breath and dove in.

"I'm going to do something that's probably never been done on this stage before. It may not look like much. But the more you think about what I'm doing here, even in the days and weeks to come, the more it's going to bug you."

Ben had written that line. It had sounded stuck-up to her, but the supportive camper crowd loved it. A couple of people whooped, and there was a smattering of applause.

"Part of what will make this demonstration so annoying is that I'm not going to be involved. I won't touch anything, choose anything, or handle anything. I'm going to rule out every possibility that anything is rigged, gimmicked, or prepared in advance."

To make her point, she walked to the side of the stage, about fifteen feet away from the table that the stagehands had wheeled out.

She looked out across the crowd of strangers. Her mouth was dry as dust. She'd always wondered what real magicians loved about performing onstage—and now, with her knees barely holding her up, she was more mystified than ever.

"I'm going to need a couple of helpers for this little experiment," she went on. "But it's important that it's somebody completely random. It can't be somebody I know. So here's how we're going to choose the volunteers: *Catch!*"

With that, she pulled two foam Nerf balls out of her skirt pockets and threw them out into the audience.

After a scramble, two kids wound up clutching bright-orange foam-rubber balls.

"Pretty random, right? But not random enough. I want the selection of these volunteers to have *nothing* to do with me. You two with the Nerf balls—throw them into the crowd *again!*"

There was a laugh, as the crowd caught on to her little game. By having two strangers throw the balls to two *other* strangers, there was no chance that Abby would wind up choosing volunteers that she'd secretly trained beforehand.

"Okay, great! You two with the Nerf balls—please join me on stage. Oh—and nice catch." She smiled, and there was a little bit of clapping.

To Abby, it looked like the two volunteers were moving at the speed of slugs; in the time it seemed to take them to come onto the stage, she thought, she could have run off the stage, hailed a taxi, and driven all the way home to Eastport.

Finally, they were with her, awaiting instructions.

Abby asked for their names—they were Joshua and Carly—and introduced them to the crowd.

"All right. First you, Joshua. On the table to your left,

you'll see a carton of a dozen hard-boiled eggs. We only need one of them. Your job is to prove to this audience that there is absolutely nothing tricky going on with any of these eggs. Go ahead: pick up a couple of them. Crack 'em with your fist. Peel off the shell. Throw a couple out to people in the audience. All I ask is that we wind up with one egg to use for the trick."

As the crowd giggled, Joshua picked up three eggs, hefted them, examined them—and then began to juggle them, showing off.

This is what I get for doing the trick at a magic camp, Abby thought.

"That's great, Joshua," she said aloud. "You get to perform in *tomorrow's* Camper Show."

The crowd cracked up. Abby felt the tiniest flutter of pride and excitement; that line Ben *hadn't* written.

Joshua cracked a few eggs on the edge of the table, split them, showed them, tossed a couple more into the crowd. The cameraman followed all of the action.

"Okay, Joshua," Abby said finally. "Are you pretty satisfied that this was a dozen ordinary eggs, and that you've wound up with one of them that you, and you alone, picked out?"

"Yes I am," said Joshua, waggling his eyebrows into the camera.

"All right. Carly, you're up next. For you, I have a little

arts-and-crafts project. Also on that table, I've brought you a dozen spools of thread, all different colors. You're going to pick one—I'm not going to pick one, or even touch one. Pick out any color you like, and break off a four-foot piece of thread."

"Okay," Carly said. She bent over to examine the thread and finally picked out a spool of dark blue.

"How's that thread look to you? Any trapdoors, mirrors, or secret assistants?"

Carly smiled at her and shook her head no. "It's just thread," she said.

"Great," Abby went on. "Can you tie one end of that thread around the middle of the ruler there? And then use the tape to fasten the other end to Joshua's egg. I'd love to help out, but I made a promise that I wouldn't get involved."

When the volunteers had finished, they had created what looked like a first-grader's science-fair project. Each of them held one end of the ruler. The egg dangled from the thread between them.

"Can you make it stop turning?" Abby asked. Joshua reached out to steady the egg. It was motionless now, except for the faintest side-to-side swinging.

"Actually, my real question is this: Can you make it *start* turning?"

Just as Carly reached toward the egg, Abby quickly added, "without touching it, without blowing on it, and without moving the ruler?"

Carly, Joshua, and the audience chuckled as they suddenly realized how difficult that would be.

"No, we can't," Joshua finally told her.

"But I can," Abby said with a smile.

And she did.

She turned to look at the egg. Then, with her fingers hidden by her long hair, she tugged at her earlobes. The great thing, as Ben had pointed out in rehearsal, was that you couldn't tell that she was pulling on her ears; it looked as though she was just massaging her temples, the perfectly normal gesture of a mind reader.

But the truth is, nobody in that audience was paying much attention to Abby and her magical gesture. Every eye was on the egg, which began to spin on the end of that thread in the most ghostly way. The giant high-definition screens revealed every speck of dust on the Scotch Tape and every tiny bit of fluff on the dark-blue thread.

And there was complete silence in the Weasley Theater.

What's going on? Abby thought, flicking her eyes away from the egg for a fraction of a second. *Don't they see it? Why don't they react?*

She knew what was happening, of course: she had just

exposed herself as a freak. It was like going on TV to brag about how loudly you can burp. The entire world of Camp Cadabra would now realize that she was a complete weirdo—and they'd laugh about her for years.

But that wasn't the worst of it. After flopping in such a big way, she'd never have a chance to find out what her dumb little power was all about. She'd never find anyone else like her, or anyone who knew anything about this kind of thing.

To the audience, it looked like Abby had forgotten what was supposed to come next. She stood there, flustered, her hand starting to shake.

"Go on, Abby!"

She looked out into the blinding darkness, but she couldn't see anyone past the third row. She had, however, recognized the voice; it was Ben's. It was enough to snap her back to earth.

"Stop it, Carly," Abby said, finally remembering how the trick was supposed to go on. "Stop it from spinning, will you?"

Carly did, using her hand. Abby made it spin again.

"No, seriously—try to make it stop," Abby said, forcing a grin.

Carly grabbed the egg, steadied it, and let go. But it started spinning again. For the first time, Abby could hear the audience coming alive, buzzing and pointing.

"All right, you guys. Now comes phase 2. I need you to shorten that thread up, so the egg is only hanging a foot down from the ruler."

The two volunteers turned the ruler over and over, winding the thread around it.

"Great! Good job. And now, how about lowering it into the water?"

The water was actually a fish tank—or, rather, the Nature Station's glass terrarium. Ben had carefully transferred the plants, the gravel, and the turtle out of it, washed out the terrarium, and then filled it with tap water. ("Presto, change-o," he'd said. "Now it's an aquarium!")

Carly and Josh stepped a couple of paces closer to the aquarium table and stood on either side. Carly steadied the egg, and then the two of them lowered it into the water.

"That's it," Abby said. "Just rest the ruler across the top."

There the egg sat, halfway down in the fish tank, completely inaccessible to air currents, utterly untouched by human hands. An egg in a tank.

The cameraman crouched down to focus his lens on the underwater egg.

"Now, we're all magicians here. You're all capable of figuring out how any trick is done. What I'd like you to do now is figure out how *this* is done."

And with that, she reached up to her earlobes again and made that egg spin in *water*. It was the creepiest darned

83

thing most of those campers and counselors had ever seen.

This time, Abby didn't have to wonder what they were thinking. The applause was immediate—and thunderous. It continued as Abby dropped her hands to her sides, and the egg slowly swam to a stop. Abby took a step backward, beaming.

She looked out into the theater, the waves of fear finally falling away. For the first time, she was able to experience the audience's reaction, and it was *awesome*. She felt like flying. She wasn't a freak anymore—she was a magician! With Ben's help, she had turned her pointless power into an actual stage illusion—and *that*, she thought, was quite a trick.

She scanned the audience, hoping to spot Ben, but the spotlights continued to blind her.

Much later, though, she would remember something that she *did* see, something she didn't think was important at the time: a line of three counselors sitting together in the second row. They were the only ones not clapping. Instead, they were bending forward in a huddle, talking fast, looking up at the egg and pointing in her direction.

CHAPTER
10
Ferd

ABBY QUICKLY DISCOVERED a great thing about performing a hit trick at Camper Show: you become a minor celebrity. When she got back to Witches 3 that night, No-H Sara and the other girls mobbed her, hugged her, high-fived her, and pelted her with questions and congratulations.

"I thought you haven't done much magic before?"

"What'd Ferd say?"

"Will you look at my trick and tell me if you think it's any good?"

"How long did you have to practice?"

"Where'd you get those Nerf balls?"

But Abby also quickly discovered a not-so-great thing

about performing a hit trick at Camper Show: the conversation turned pretty quickly to how she did it.

"Hey, so how does the trick work?"

"Yeah, how'd you do it?"

"What's the secret?"

"Can you teach me?"

"Come on, you can tell us. We're your best friends!"

Unfortunately, she couldn't tell them. Oh, she would have told them the secret of the trick—if there were one to tell. But what do you say when you don't even know how it works yourself?

So Abby froze, unable to say anything at all. "Well, it's—it's kind of complicated," she managed in a small voice.

Fortunately, Claudia the counselor caught her panic-stricken look and stepped in to help. "Come on, witchezzzz," she said matter-of-factly, "There'll be time for that later. It's already past lights-out time. Who's first for the outdoor shower?"

And just like that, the party broke up. Little No-H Sara was the last to leave Abby's side—"You're gonna tell me how you did that, girl!" she said with an evil look—and then it was over.

In the morning, on the way to breakfast, everybody seemed to recognize Abby. Nobody had the first clue what her name was, but everybody who'd been at the show high-fived her, gave her a thumbs-up, or at least smiled as they passed. The whole feeling of Camp Cadabra had changed.

She didn't see Ben until Impromptu class that morning. As soon as he loped into the room, he broke into a huge smile and gave her a quick, clumsy hug. "You did great," he said.

"It was your idea," she countered.

"Yeah, but it's your power." He seemed convinced at last.

When Ferd entered the room, once again wearing a huge Hawaiian shirt, the class began. At last, Abby could sink back into the routine of being nobody special.

But it didn't last long.

Ferd's class that day, as often happened, had more to do with presentation and style than with the step-by-steps for performing one particular trick. At the end of the class, Ferd wrapped up by saying: "And this, my people, is my final word of advice to you in your blossoming impromptu career: Know when to stop. A magician who performs just one unforgettable effect is a genius; a magician who performs just one too many is a fool. Be good, my people. Now be off."

As the campers began rounding up their stuff and

putting the props back in the prop baskets, he added: "All but you, Miss Carnelia. I'd like a word, if you will."

Abby looked up, startled. What on earth would Ferd want with her?

She looked at Ben, who looked back at her with the same *what-the-heck?* look.

"Don't worry. He won't bite," he whispered. "Just don't let him give you any fashion tips."

As the room cleared, Abby stepped up to the front of the room. "Did—did you want to see me?"

Ferd opened a drawer and pulled out a clipboard. He stepped over to one of the tables and gestured toward a chair for her. "Please."

He pulled out a chair across from her and lowered his substantial body onto it with an audible sigh. He laid his palms flat on the black stone tabletop.

"Miss Carnelia. That was quite a performance last night," he began.

"Thank you," she said.

"May I have a word with you about your little demonstration?"

"Oh—okay," she said, uncertainly.

"Miss Carnelia, you may consider me little more than an eccentric camp counselor with a ponytail and an emphatic mode of dialectic."

Abby's face told him that she didn't understand.

"That is to say, I talk funny. Or so I have been told by campers, on occasion."

"I think you talk fine," said Abby, truthfully.

"Despite the peculiarities of my speech," Ferd went on, "here's something you may not realize: I may know the art of legerdemain better than anyone you're likely to meet for some time. As a teenager, I took first place in close-up at the National Young Magicians' Competition—three years in a row."

One pudgy finger stabbed the table for emphasis with each word.

"The point is, I know a thing or two about the art." He cleared his throat. "Now then."

To Abby's total surprise, Ferd reached into a small props bag and extracted an egg.

"I wish to offer you some suggestions," he said, gently placing the egg on the hard black table.

Abby couldn't believe her ears. "That's why you wanted to see me?"

"Absolutely. This is my purpose in life, Miss Carnelia: to foster the most promising magicians, to help them blossom, to guide them along their paths. And I believe that perhaps I can improve the impact of your effect. Would you do me the honor?" He gestured toward the egg. "Please. Proceed."

Deep inside, Abby had a queasy feeling, as though the train of her life was about to jump off its tracks. But she didn't have much of a choice.

"Okay, so I have this egg," she began. "And I can make it spin when I pull on my earlobes."

And she did.

Ferd's face didn't change at all. After a moment, he looked up at her.

"That's quite remarkable, actually. I can't remember anyone doing this particular effect before. If I may be so bold: what else can you show me?"

She looked at him. "You mean, like, another trick?"

He nodded, smiled, and looked at her expectantly. Abby stared down at the table.

"That's pretty much it, at this point," she finally said. "I don't really have anything else. I mean, that's ready."

"This is your only effect?" he said, his eyes drilling into her.

She looked up. "Well, yeah. I'm kind of new at magic."

"Fine—fine. Then I'll tell you what: let's work on your egg demonstration, shall we? I believe that we should work on the trigger. If I may speak frankly, the trigger is much too subtle. When you reach into your hair in that way, the audience can't see what you're doing. And the trigger ges-ture is not even directed toward the prop. Massaging the temples might pass in a mentalism routine. But here, it just looks like you have a headache."

Abby was stunned—and a little annoyed. Her face showed it.

"Miss Carnelia," Ferd added hurriedly. "My intent is not to insult or belittle your efforts here. But I feel that you could benefit from the fruits of my experience. If you'd prefer not to hear it, then I shall make myself scarce and ask your forgiveness. Now, shall I continue, or not?"

She took a deep breath, and then nodded.

Ferd reached out and fingered the egg on the table.

"Let's try it again, shall we? With a different trigger, now. Show me something more visible. More direct." He smiled and leaned back.

Once again, Abby stared hard at the table.

After a moment, Ferd leaned over, rolled the egg a few inches closer to Abby, steadied it, and gestured with his hand.

"*Let's see it again,*" he said deliberately.

Abby unsteadily reached for her earlobes again. But Ferd interrupted.

"No! Not the ears. I want you to find a *different* trigger!"

Abby couldn't look him in the eye. "I—I can't."

Strangely enough, that seemed to be just the answer Ferd was hoping to hear. He suddenly seemed to be incredibly fascinated. His round body seemed to swell up as his juices began flowing.

"Miss Carnelia. Are you telling me that the effect won't work if you choose a different trigger?"

For the longest time, Abby had looked forward to sharing her secret with someone who really knew about magic. That, after all, was why she was here. This should have been a moment of triumph, joy, and happiness.

But instead, Ferd was creeping her out. She wasn't sure how comfortable she was spilling her guts to him.

"Aha—evidently not," Ferd went on. "Then let me ask you another question. In the name of our mutual interest in this great art, would you consider revealing your method?"

"My—method?"

"Tell me how you do it," Ferd said, his face intense. He was leaning forward so far, she could feel his breath. Without even being aware of it, she was pushing herself back in her chair as far as she could go.

"Come on, Abby. Tell me. Tell me what the *earlobes* have to do with the *egg*. Tell me how the egg spins!"

This guy is losing it, she thought. Ferd persisted. "Tell me how your family treats you when you perform this effect!"

It was as though he could see right through her.

"Tell me *how long you've had this power.*"

Abby's jaw dropped. She gripped the sides of her chair so hard that her knuckles went white.

"How—how do you *know* that?" was all she could manage. She kept her grip on the sides of her chair.

He nodded, leaning back at last, and beamed broadly, a big happy bullfrog.

"Abby. Listen to me. I worked to build this camp. I helped to design it. Before that, I ran the magic programs at two other performing arts camps. I've trained hundreds of magicians. I've watched hundreds more. I spend my time monitoring the magic chat rooms on the Internet. And I've heard about . . . certain . . . *special* kids."

Abby felt a chill go down her spine.

"Now, maybe you have a method and you're just not telling me. But maybe, just maybe, you're something special. Maybe you have more than a trick here." He paused, watching her. "And the fact that you have completely stopped breathing tells me that I'm right."

Abby smiled nervously and, flustered, shook her head as though to break a spell. This was why she was here, wasn't it? To find someone who knew something about her power? Then why did she feel so threatened?

"Okay, you're right," she said. "I just found out about it a couple of months ago. I was peeling some hard-boiled eggs. I'm actually here because the ad said I'd learn about paranormal abilities."

She looked up at him, as though to say, *and now it's your move.*

93

Ferd smiled, closing his eyes briefly.

"This is beautiful, Abby," he said with satisfaction. "It's always an honor to meet someone with your abilities. I want you to know that I'll keep our relationship in complete confidence; the other kids don't need to know that I'm working with you."

It occurred to Abby that Ferd's manner was slowly changing. He was calling her "Abby" now, instead of "Miss Carnelia." And he wasn't talking so weirdly anymore. *He's probably forgetting to do that,* she thought.

"And so if you're willing," Ferd concluded, "I'd love for you to consider me your sounding board, your great listener, your friend. I want you to tell me everything you know about your gift." He picked up his clipboard and held it tightly, pen poised over the paper.

So Abby Carnelia took a deep breath and told her story, in more detail than she'd ever told it to anyone. Ferd took a lot of notes, raised his eyebrows a few times, said a lot of "Hmmmmm!"s. He, at least, was loving every minute of it.

When she'd finished, Ferd sat there for a moment, studying his notes. "Abby, Abby, Abby," was all he said.

"What?" she asked. She was feeling a little frustrated that she was the one doing all the talking. *He* was supposed to be the expert.

"Do you know what I have?" she asked him, as though he were a doctor. "I mean, why I have it? Do you know where it came from? Does anyone else have it?"

Ferd stared at her for an uncomfortable amount of time before he finally spoke.

"We don't know why you have it, Abby," he said finally. "We don't know how you do it, or where you got it, or when you got it—or even when you won't have it anymore."

Abby blinked. That was something that had never occurred to her before.

"But I can definitely answer your last question. Does anybody else have a power like yours? The answer is yes, Abby. There are others."

Abby's eyes went wide.

Ferd laid his clipboard on the table and clasped his hands.

"And I'd like for you to meet them."

"It was you, Ben. You did it!"

Abby ran up to her bewildered friend and pounded his shoulder happily with both fists. Illusion Building was just ending, and Abby knew she'd find him there. It was a clear, cool day, and Abby felt as high as the puffy white clouds.

"It wasn't me, I swear!" he said, grinning and tossing the bangs out of his eyes. "Whatever went wrong, I wasn't there."

Abby pushed him backward so that he plopped down onto a not-yet-painted illusion cabinet that lay on its side in the sawdust.

"No, you did. You helped me find what I came here for," she beamed, panting.

"Whoa there, bronco. Maybe you should slow down and tell me what the heck you're talking about." He patted an empty place on the cabinet next to him.

But Abby couldn't sit still. She paced in front of him, gesturing with her hands.

"Listen, ever since I discovered this thing I can do, it's driven me crazy. I mean, it makes me feel like a freak. And nobody can explain it. Nobody has any idea how it's happening, or what it means, or *anything*. And maybe you think it'd be cool to have a real power, even if it's a really, really stupid power, but it's not. It's not that cool. It makes me feel lonely. I don't *like* being the only weirdo on earth!"

Ben leaned back on his elbows. "Well, there are a *few* other weirdos around here," he said with a half smile. "But okay, go on."

"Okay. So you want to know what Ferd wanted to see me about after class this morning?"

He thought for a minute. "He wanted to borrow one of your hair doodads for his ponytail?"

"Funny. No. He told me that they've found other kids with pointless little powers. It's really rare, but they're out there."

Ben straightened up, his face suddenly open and intent. "You're kidding me."

"No! And I'm invited to go to this sort of super camp, where these, like, famous genius experts are going to help us figure out what we have! Like work with us, help us expand our powers, meet these famous magicians and stuff."

Ben was having trouble taking it all in. "You and these other kids? How—I mean, like—well, okay. Where is this place?"

Abby finally contained herself enough to stop pacing. She pushed a tray of pliers and screwdrivers farther down the cabinet to make room and then sat down next to Ben. "I don't know. Pennsylvania or something. But isn't that so cool? I'm supposed to call my parents after lunch and tell them."

He cocked an eyebrow at her. "You seem pretty excited."

"Well, this is what I wanted. This is why I came to magic camp! Not to learn tricks—to learn about my power. And it was you! It was your idea to do Camper

Show. You said maybe it would get somebody's attention, and it did!"

"Well, you're welcome. It sounds like a total blast." He turned his face up to scan the cotton-ball clouds, trying to make sense of what he was hearing. "When do you leave?"

"On Saturday. We're driving. Nine hours in a van." She squeezed her eyes closed for a moment, and then added, "I'm a little scared."

He studied her face. "Nah, don't be scared. Be excited. Be happy. It's going to be awesome. I kind of wish I could go! But hey—looks like only a select few get picked for Super Camp. Mere magic rock stars like me don't qualify."

He stood up and stretched. "Listen, Abby Carnelia. I'm happy for you. But it's kind of a shame you're leaving halfway through Camp Cadabra. It's been fun knowing you. Send me an e-mail or two from Super Camp, will you?"

She smiled at him. "I promise."

As it turned out, she never did send Ben any e-mail.

"BILL!!! It's Abby on the phone!"

Mrs. Carnelia leaned on the second-floor railing, shouting downstairs. "Ryan, run and get your dad, will you? Abby's calling from camp."

Ryan scampered downstairs, and Mrs. Carnelia retreated to the bedroom with the cordless phone. She sat on the bed.

"How *are* you, darling? We got your e-mail about being selected to be in the magic show in front of the whole camp—that's wonderful! How did it go?"

"I wasn't *selected*, Mom. Anyone can be in it. Whoever wants to be," Abby replied. "Anyway, it went great. It went really well."

She was in the Camp Cadabra offices, where Ferd had encouraged her to make a phone call home about his offer. Ferd himself was hovering nearby, pretending to flip through some magic magazines on the office coffee table but staying within listening range. Abby would have preferred some privacy, but at least he'd be nearby if there were any questions.

"Beetling?" It was Mr. Carnelia's voice, picking up another line.

"Hi, Dad!" said Abby. "How's everything at home?"

"In the five days since you left? Oh, everything's *completely* different now," he joked.

"I got a toad!!" An unmistakable squeaky voice chimed in from yet another phone in the Carnelia house.

"Hi, Ry," said Abby. "That's great. Where'd you get it?"

"Found it at camp," he said. "He's my new pet. His name is Barfy."

99

"He's taking that thing right back to camp tomorrow morning," Mrs. Carnelia added quickly. "We're not a family that's good with pets. Especially ones that require live insects as food."

Abby smiled and leaned back on the office couch. "Well, that's great, Ry," she said. "Sounds like you like your camp."

"It's *wicked!*" shouted Ryan into the phone. "You should go there next year! If you're not too old and stuff."

"I'll think about it," Abby said.

"To what do we owe the pleasure of this call?" asked her father. "Does the Abbster crave the sound of our mellifluous voices?"

"No, not really," said Abby. "I mean yeah, of course. But I'm supposed to ask you for permission for something. They're going to send you some forms you have to fill out, and I'm supposed to explain what it's all about."

"Sure," said her mom. "What's going on?"

"Okay, well, you know about Camp Cadabra, right? You know there's more than one of them around the country," she began.

"Right."

"Okay, well, I guess they also have this—this, like, super camp. And they invite just a few people, like a couple campers, from each of the regular camps, to go hang out at the super camp. It's for people who are really, really talented, and you get to work with some of the most famous people in magic. And it's free and everything—they pay for everything."

Abby was closing her eyes tight. She wasn't lying, at least not exactly; there *was* a super camp, and there *were* only a couple people from each camp who got to go there. At least that's what Ferd had said.

But she was leaving out one small detail: that the people chosen to visit the super camp weren't just talented magicians—they were, according to Ferd, people with powers like hers. Considering how complicated it had been trying to explain her power to her family in the first place, Abby thought that it might be best if she left out that aspect of the super camp.

Abby's mother was impressed. "And you got picked?"

"Well, yeah, pretty much," Abby responded. "It's in Pennsylvania somewhere."

"Pennsylvania!" she heard her dad proclaim. "From upper New Hampshire? Ye gods! That's some field trip."

"I think it's wonderful, Abby," said her mom. "For them to choose you over all those kids who've been doing magic since they were little? That's a real honor!"

They didn't pick me, Abby thought. *My power picked me.*

But all she said was, "Yeah, I'm pretty psyched."

"When do you go, Ab?" asked Mr. Carnelia.

"In a couple days," she said. "I'd have to skip the rest of the regular camp, and the big show at the end, and stuff like that. But it seems like it'd be fun in its own way, you know?"

"Of course it will," said her mom. "I'm so proud of you. It's just that—well, I have a lot of questions, honey. It's a little peculiar for them to pluck you out of one camp and take you to another halfway through, isn't it?"

"Mom! Don't go all worrywart. They're going to send you a bunch of brochures and forms and stuff like that. You can ask 'em anything you want. But it's totally fine. I'm a big girl; I can handle a drive to Pennsylvania."

"That you can, McAbbister," boomed her dad. "That you can. Have them send over whatever the forms are, and we'll get them filled out. And find out if there's any kind of extra fee, so I can send a check."

"No, Dad, I told you. It's totally free."

"How can they afford to run it for free?" said Mrs. Carnelia. "Camp Cadabra is cheap enough as it is! Honey, just ask them to make sure there's not some kind of extra cost. And don't make any promises until we've seen those brochures."

"Okay, Mom," Abby said. "I will."

They chatted some more, exchanged news and gossip, promised to e-mail often, and then said goodbye.

Abby handed the phone back to Ferd, who seemed pleased.

"It's all set?" he asked.

"They're basically fine with it," she said, standing.

"That's splendid, Miss Carnelia," said Ferd. "Prepare yourself for the adventure of a lifetime."

CHAPTER
11
Van

On the morning she was supposed to leave for super camp, Abby sat on the floor of Witches 3, packing up her duffel bag. No-H Sara didn't exactly help her pack, but did lend emotional support. All right, she didn't exactly do that either. But she did keep Abby company.

"I just don't get why it's *you*," Sara said, flouncing onto Abby's deep, soft mattress. "I mean, your egg thing was amazing, totally amazing. But I mean, did you see that kid's fire trick last night? It was like *crazy!*"

Abby smiled as she rolled up a pair of socks. "Thanks for the vote of confidence," she said sardonically.

"No, no, no, no, no, I didn't mean it *that* way. I'm just saying—why not him, too? It's like, 'Hmmm. Spin an egg? Or make fire come out of your fingers?' You know?"

"When are you going to sign up for Camper Show?" asked Abby. She had noticed that although No-H Sara was very good at critiquing other people's performances, she hadn't done much in the way of performing herself.

"Next week for sure," Sara said.

Abby stood up, checked the bureau drawers, looked under her bed, and took a last look in the bathroom, just to make sure she had everything.

"I guess that's it," she announced. She picked up one end of her duffel bag, tipping it onto its back wheels. "I'm gonna head down to the parking lot."

Sara sprang out of the bed and threw her arms around Abby. "Bye, Abby!" she said. "Have a great time, and send a lot of e-mail!"

Abby returned the hug. "I will," she promised, and she turned to go.

Sara put her hand on Abby's shoulder. "Oh—and Abby?"

"Yeah?"

Sara looked up tenderly into Abby's face, her blond frizzy hair like cotton candy in the morning sun.

"Can I have your bunk? Mine has a lump."

Abby grinned. "Go for it," she said.

And with that, she rolled out of Witches 3 forever.

⁂

When Abby arrived at the parking lot, she saw the bright red Camp Cadabra van waiting with its rear doors thrown open for luggage, and its side doors flung open for passengers. As she approached, she saw one familiar sight—Ferd's expansive body and bouncing ponytail—and two campers she didn't recognize.

"Hi!" she said as she arrived, slightly out of breath.

"Ah, yes, Miss Carnelia," said Ferd grandly. "Pleased to see you on time and ready to roll. Do you know your fellow camp mates Richard and Eliza?"

"It's *Ricky*," corrected the short boy with the perfectly spherical head. Seriously. If he had been wearing a T-shirt with a big zigzag on it, you would have thought he was Charlie Brown.

He stuck out his hand, which was how he had been introducing himself to people since he was three years old.

"Hi, I'm Abby," she said, shaking his sweaty hand delicately.

"That's funny," Ricky responded.

She didn't get it. "My name?"

"Abby Cadabra. Get it?"

She got it. She rewarded him with one-third of a smile.

"Hello, Abby Cadabra. I'm Eliza," said Eliza.

Her dominant color was orange. Red hair, red lipstick, lots of freckles, and an orange-and-red tie-dyed T-shirt. A *big* T-shirt, size XXXXXXXL, about six hundred times too big for her. It could have fit Abby's entire family.

They stood there for a moment, awkwardly glancing around.

"What cabin you in?" said Eliza.

"Witches 3?" said Abby helpfully. "How 'bout you?"

"Witches 2," said Eliza.

"Ah."

"What grade are you guys?"

"Going into seventh," said Abby. "Me, too," said Eliza. "What about you?"

"Eighth," said Ricky.

"You're going into eighth grade?" Eliza asked, looking at him skeptically. Ricky's very round head came up almost to her shoulder.

"I skipped a year," was all he said.

Ferd had been pacing a few yards away, but now he returned to the van. "Climb aboard," he told them. "We must commence our journey posthaste."

As the three campers climbed into the van, Ferd dragged their bags around and loaded them into the back. Abby and Eliza shared the first bench seat, behind the driver's seat; Ricky took the row behind that.

Abby couldn't stand the silence. Weren't these exactly the people she'd dreamed of knowing—other people with powers? Didn't they have a world of notes to compare? Shouldn't they all be talking at once?

It was as though there were an elephant in the room, and nobody was talking about it.

She was just summoning her courage to ask a couple of more—well, *personal* questions of Eliza and Ricky, when the driver's door snapped open. Ferd hauled himself into the driver's seat and put the key into the ignition. "My people, we have a nine-hour drive before us. This would be a fine opportunity to avail yourselves of the bathroom facilities. Anybody?"

Nobody said anything.

"Excellent then! Let's blow this clambake," he said. He started the van.

Suddenly, a metallic banging came from the back of the van. Somebody was trying to get Ferd's attention.

All three kids turned to see who it was. Through the rear window, they could see a red T-shirt. It was a male counselor, yelling something.

"What impeccable timing," said Ferd.

The rear doors flew open, and the red-shirted counselor hauled one more duffel bag into the back.

"Our final passenger has arrived," Ferd said.

The rear doors closed. The side door opened. The last passenger climbed in.

It was Ben.

CHAPTER
12
Ricky

"**B**EN!" **ABBY YELPED,** a smile growing. "What—what are you doing here?"

He squeezed past her and swung into the seat behind her.

"Same as you," he grinned. "Going for a super-long van ride."

Abby was completely confused.

"Buckle up, my people," said Ferd at the wheel. "That's the full load. *Vámanos!*"

The van pulled forward with a crunch of gravel. After a moment, it was bumping along the piney road out of camp.

Abby stole a look back at Ben over her shoulder. He grinned back at her through his stringy bangs and, when he was sure nobody else was looking, quickly signaled her by putting his finger to his lips in a *Shhhh!* motion.

"As long as there's no conversation back there," Ferd said after a minute, "then I intend to fill the silence with a bit of musical entertainment." With one hand, he reached out on the seat next to him, feeling for his CD case. "I have the complete works of Beethoven played on bag-pipes."

There was an instant reaction.

"Hi, I'm Ricky!" "I'm Ben." "You're Abby, right?" "I call her Abby Cadabra." "I'm Eliza." "Nice to meet you."

Ferd shook his head in mock disappointment. "You don't like classical? You young people today have no taste at all."

"So, I mean . . ." Abby began. "Do you guys all have—"

She looked from face to face, hoping that somebody, *anybody*, would start explaining what was going on here. But she didn't want to dive right in and start talking about how she had a true magical power. That hadn't worked out so great the last time she told someone.

"Special talents?" It was Ricky, finishing her sentence.

She turned. "Yeah!" she said. "Do you?"

"Kinda," he said. He looked around at the others, nervously.

"Tell us!" said Eliza.

Ricky looked down at his lap, too embarrassed to speak.

"Don't be shy, dude," Ben chimed gently.

"Ladies and gentlemen," said Ferd suddenly. "You should know that you'll be spending the next week together—as a unit, as it were. You have been selected for your mutual abilities. So it would be my suggestion that you cherish your similarity. Nobody will make fun of you here, my people. You're among friends."

"So," said Eliza. "Will you tell us about yourself, Ricky?"

He looked up. "What do you want to know?"

"At least tell us all the boring stuff. How old you are, brothers and sisters, all that junk," Abby said.

"I'm twelve. I have three older sisters. I live in New York City. I have a rat."

"A rat?" said Eliza.

"Yeah. A pet," said Ricky. "What's wrong with that?"

"It's just gross," said Eliza.

"How's it any grosser than a mouse?" asked Ricky, annoyed. "It's just a big mouse."

Ben, who was still new to the concept that there might be people with actual supernatural powers, was leaning forward and listening hard.

"Tell us about your magic, Ricky," he said.

"Well, I've been doing magic shows since I was in

seventh grade. I do birthday parties sometimes. I'm learning balloon twisting, too. The little kids really like that."

Abby and Ben exchanged a look. Ricky was avoiding the subject.

"Do you have . . . you know, one *special* trick?" Abby asked.

"I'm not supposed to talk about it. My mom says it only gets me in trouble."

"Hey, I know," said Ben. "Abby, why don't you tell these guys about your power, and then everybody else can go next?"

Abby wasn't especially thrilled about going first; she had grown so used to keeping her freakiness a secret that it was almost second nature to hide it. Still, she'd had a little practice—she'd told Morgan, and Ben, and Ferd, and the world hadn't ended.

So she looked out the window a moment, took a breath, and then told the whole story. From the beginning. Salad. Ryan. The library. Her dad. Summer camp. Camper Show.

The other kids were completely absorbed, twisted in their seat belts to listen. Even Ben was rapt; he hadn't heard her whole story in such detail.

". . . and so Ferd said that he wanted me to meet other

kids with real powers," Abby concluded. "And I think he means you guys!"

Eliza was staring at her. "That's it? That's all you can do . . . spin an egg?"

"Well, yeah." She met Eliza's gaze. "I didn't pick this power, you know. It is what it is."

"My turn!" The others turned to look at Ricky. Now that Abby had gone first, Ricky was a lot more confident.

"Tell! Tell!" said Eliza.

"Well, okay, what I didn't really tell you is that I have a power, too. I actually had it before I ever got into magic. I mean, you know—magic tricks."

Abby nodded, encouraging him.

"Okay. So this one time? I was in Spanish class?"

Ricky had a way of making his voice go up at the end of sentences, so it sounded like he was asking questions when he actually wasn't.

"And I was with my friend Tad. We were supposed to be paired up together, the whole class, like, buddied up. We were supposed to practice counting in Spanish, to learn how to say the numbers. Tad lives two houses down from me on my street, so we've been friends for, like, ever. We always buddy up when we're supposed to pick a practice buddy. Except this one time? Like in sixth grade? I got *so* mad at him. He borrowed my bike, and like, totally crashed it. He said he didn't. He said he never did. But I could tell, because the little thing you push to ring the bell wouldn't move anymore, and also the back brakes, you had to squeeze really, really hard to make 'em work?"

"Go on," said Ben, hoping to nudge Ricky back to the magic part of the story.

"Okay. So anyway, we're practicing counting to a hundred. And the teacher, Mr. Lebowitz, he said to practice for five minutes, and then he stepped out of the room. He does that sometimes. We don't know what he does when he does that. Some kids think he just has to go to the bathroom a lot. But there's this one kid? Thornton? He thinks Mr. Lebowitz has a secret girlfriend in the school, like another teacher. And that every time he sneaks out of Spanish, he goes and meets her in the teacher's lounge and *kisses* her!"

Ricky cracked himself up, his face like a grinning grapefruit.

"So what happened in Spanish that day?" Abby prodded.

"Well, anyway, Mr. Lebowitz was out of the room, and so everybody started to get a little silly. Tad starts saying the numbers like a robot. '*Uno . . . dos . . . tres . . . cuatro . . .*'"

Ricky was imitating his friend, speaking in a dull, electronic, monotone voice.

"And so then I started counting like a big fat opera singer." And Ricky demonstrated, singing high and warbled.

" 'Unooooooo! Doooo-ooos! Treee-eee-eeees!' It was so funny!"

The other kids laughed politely, but Abby kept wondering if there was going to be an end to this story.

"And then Tad, he started counting by twos, like *dos, cuatro, seis, ocho.* You know, like two, four, six, eight. Only he was doing it like Darth Vader, with all these, like breathing sounds in between. He is *such* a *Star Wars* freak. You can't believe his room! He's got every single action figure, in like three different sizes. He has this life-size R2-D2 that really works! He can make it move with a remote control. You press this one button, and it makes all the little R2-D2 noises. You know what Tad's birthday party is? It's a *Star Wars* birthday party *every year.* Every single year since he was four!"

"Impressive," said Eliza, entirely unimpressed.

"What about the magic, Ricky?" prodded Ben.

"Okay, right. So after he did the Darth Vader sounds, I started saying the numbers backward. Not like spelled backward or counting backward, I mean *talking like this.*"

And when he said "talking like this," Ricky did that creepy thing that boys sometimes do where they *breathe in* while they're talking. They actually speak while they're inhaling. It made his voice sound sort of watery, old, and raspy. But anyway, creepy.

"And Thornton? He was sitting right by the window, and I look over, and he's drawing on the window. You know how you can fog up the glass on a window? Like if you lean right up to it and breathe on it? There was a fogged-up place on the window, and he was writing his initials in it."

Ricky stopped, and looked around for effect.

"See?"

Abby didn't. "What do you mean?"

"He didn't fog up the window! He was writing in the fogged-up place with his finger, but he didn't breathe on it. He didn't fog up the window!"

Ben couldn't help thinking that Ricky had somehow left out a piece of the story; he didn't get it at all.

"Well, *someone* must have fogged it up, right?" he said.

"I know! That's what I'm telling you!" said Ricky, getting frustrated. "I did it! I fogged that window. By counting in Spanish by twos breathing in!"

Abby looked at Ben with a face that said, *Is this kid for real?*

Eliza was looking at him with one cocked eyebrow. "So let me get this straight. Your power is that you can fog up a window? By counting in Spanish with that weird voice?"

Ricky nodded. "By twos. I have to count by twos."

117

Eliza rolled her eyes and turned to face the front of the van, as though to say, *I'm done with this conversation.*

"How did you know?" asked Abby. "How did you know it was you?"

"Because," Ricky said. "I was watching Thornton writing with his finger, and I did it again. I started over at *dos.* And I saw another foggy place fog up on the window right next to the first one. And the thing is, I wasn't even close to the window! I was sitting with Tad, like across the whole room from it. And so I did it again, and a couple more times. I was totally freaking out? So I told Tad to watch the window, too? And he did, and I did the trick, and told him how I was making the window fog up, but he didn't believe me. He told me that Thornton was just breathing on the window, since he was sitting next to it. So I was mad. So you know what I did?"

Abby shook her head no.

"I fogged up his glasses! It was almost by accident. I just looked right at them, and counted again by twos— *dos! cuatro! seis!*—and they fogged right up, like the bathroom mirror. It was so great! And he's like, 'HEY!' And he had to take them off to wipe them on his shirt. And he's like, 'Don't breathe on my glasses. That's disgusting,' and I'm like, 'Okay, sorry.' But then he puts them back on again and I pushed my chair wayyyy back so I was really far from him. And I'm like, 'I'll just sit over here so I won't accidentally breathe on your glasses, okay?' And he's like, 'That's better!' So then he goes, 'Okay, my turn. Who am I being?' And he was gonna start counting again in another funny voice. Except I interrupted him and said, 'No, it's still my turn. I didn't get to a hundred.' And so I looked right at his glasses and did it again! He was so mad! It was so funny!"

Ricky was stomping his feet on the floor of the van with excitement.

There was a pause, and then Eliza spoke. "So do it."

"What?" said Ricky.

"Let's see it. Fog up my window." Eliza tapped the van window beside her.

Abby thought that Eliza was being rude, but Ricky was perfectly cheerful about it. "Okay, sure," he said.

There wasn't much to it. Using that weird inhaling-voice thing, he said, "Dos, cuatro, seis, ocho, diez." It sounded a little like a seal barking.

A round patch of Eliza's window, about the size of a cookie, fogged up as though someone had breathed on it. Ricky was a few feet away, way too far for him to have done it with his breath.

Eliza cocked an eyebrow. "Not bad," she said. She couldn't resist; she put her finger up to the window and drew a fancy script E in the foggy patch, which was already starting to fade away, from the outside in.

"Does it work when you don't use that weird voice?" she asked.

"Nope."

"What about counting not by twos? What if you just count one, two, three in Spanish?"

"Nope," Ricky said again. "It only works this way."

Abby would have found his trigger hilarious—if hers weren't equally peculiar. Mostly, she was delighted to discover that his power was just as useless and unimportant as her own. She imagined that he'd gone through many of the same experiences and feelings.

"It's amazing, Ricky," she told him, turning from the foggy patch to look back at Ricky. "What does your family think?"

Ricky turned his head to look out at the passing scenery, which was hilly and green. "My sisters all think it's just a magic trick. But my parents were really upset. They thought there was something wrong with me. They took me to a psychiatrist."

"And what did he say?"

"She. She asked a bunch of questions, but couldn't figure out what my little fogged-glass thing had to do with my personality or whatever. I think she was a little scared.

Anyway, she said I should see a doctor. So we went and saw a doctor, and he did about a million tests and finally said there was nothing wrong with me. My parents kept telling him that they had to do something, so he said if they were still worried, they should take me to see a priest."

"A priest?" Ben chimed in. "They thought it was something religious?"

"They thought maybe I needed an exorcism," Ricky said solemnly. "You know, like in the movies. Where evil spirits take over your body, and a priest does a special ceremony to get 'em out."

"So did they try that?" asked Eliza.

"Well, they were gonna. My parents took me to see this old priest guy on the Upper West Side. He lived in this little tiny apartment, like you wouldn't believe how small it was. The bathtub is in the kitchen! Anyway, this guy asked a ton of questions that had nothing to do with me, like did I have visions, did I ever hear voices, did I scream in my sleep, did I ever have blackouts where I just can't remember what happened in the last few hours, did I ever feel compelled to do something evil, all this stuff. I told him no, not any of those things. Only that I can fog up glass. He made me leave the room so he could talk to my parents, but later on, they told me what he said anyway."

"What?" Abby asked.

"He said that an exorcism wouldn't do any good because I'm not actually possessed by any evil spirits. He didn't know how to explain my trick, but he was positive that there's nothing in the Bible about people fogging up windows."

Eliza snorted. "Surprise, surprise," she said.

"How did you get picked for this trip?" Abby said. Of course, *she* had gotten noticed by performing at Camper Show. But she didn't remember Ricky doing any on-stage performances where the counselors might have noticed him.

"Oh, it was kinda weird," he replied, getting back into storytelling mode. "So this one night? In our cabin? It was after lights-out, and we were just whispering back and forth, me and this kid who's in the bed across from me? We could see a light shining through one of the windows in our cabin, and I was gonna see if I could make him freak out. I told him there was a ghost who likes to hang around our cabin, a Spanish ghost, who speaks Spanish and stuff, and I told him I could make the ghost appear. I told him to watch the light through the window really closely, and see if he could see the ghost passing in front of it. And so I started making all kinds of weird noises and sounds, like really quietly and whispery, just saying weird words and stuff? And in the middle of it, I did my Spanish counting. And the glass fogged up, all the way across the cabin, and it looked just like some ghost was passing in front of the light out there."

"Whoa," breathed Ben, admiring the prank.

"Oh, yeah, it rocked," said Ricky proudly.

"Did it scare the other kid?" Abby asked.

"Oh man, he started crying! He was totally completely scared. And he's fourteen! He gets out of bed and goes and wakes up our counselor and tells him what happened. And he's all, like, 'Don't worry, little guy, it's just a trick, it's not real, there's no ghosts, go back to sleep.' But the next day, our counselor came over and talked to me, and I showed him how I did it? And I guess that was it. After lunch, he took me to meet this other counselor, and he asked me if I wanted to go to super camp. And I said, sure."

"Who was it, Ricky? Who was the other counselor?" asked Ben.

"You know. Him," he said.

He was pointing at Ferd.

CHAPTER
13
Eliza

THE CAMP CADABRA VAN WAS ROOMY AND MODERN, but it wasn't designed for all-day drives. The seat benches made your butt sore after a couple of hours. As a result, the kids kept shifting positions, crossing and uncrossing their legs, turning around and leaning on the seat backs, and generally avoiding holding the same position for too long.

Fortunately, Ferd made plenty of stops, too, for bathroom breaks, snacks, and lunch.

At around noon, they picked up some Tex-Mex Express, to go, and piled back into the van. As they started chomping their burritos and tacos, Ricky reminded them that not everybody had told their stories yet.

"Like Eliza," he said, with a stringy scrap of lettuce

hanging from the corner of his mouth. "I wanna know what your power is."

From the back seat, most of what he'd seen of Eliza was the back of her crinkly red hair; she had spent most of the ride listening to the conversation, but looking out the window, too.

"I don't know. It's private," Eliza said without even turning around.

"Aw, *come* on!" Ricky exclaimed. "I told you about mine!"

"Yeah, really, Eliza," Abby added. "I thought we had a pact. I thought we're a team."

"Throw us a crumb, Eliza," added Ben from the back seat.

Even Ferd chimed in. "Fair's fair, little lady," he said. Abby was astonished, because Ferd had been wearing earbuds for the whole ride. She had figured that he'd been lost in his world of classical bagpipe music.

Eliza sniffed. "What do you want to know?"

"What's your *power?*" said Ricky impatiently.

"Fine," she said, a little standoffishly. She looked out the window and pretended to be bored. They were passing through a town. Like so many American towns, it had a main drag, a strip of shops and restaurants where, if you were really, really hungry, you could eat at Wendy's, McDonald's, Taco Bell, KFC, *and* Friendly's without having to walk more than half a mile.

Finally, after a moment, Eliza said: "I can levitate."

What? Abby thought. She turned to look at Ben, who was equally shocked. She'd thought that all of these powers would turn out to be pointless little silly things like hers—and like Ricky's.

But levitation? Floating in the air? That would be another story. That'd be more like the magic you read about or see movies about. *Real* magic. That would be historic! People had been dreaming about flying for thousands of years. And there was someone in the van who could do it!

"Whoooooooaaaa," breathed Ricky. "Like, for real? Like, rising in the air?"

Ben was also having trouble with the concept. It had been hard enough for him to believe in Abby's teeny-tiny power. Even Ricky's power was hard for him to swallow; his brain was scrambling to figure out what this was all about.

But levitating was a completely different level of freakiness. That wouldn't be just *bending* the laws of nature, like making an egg spin or fogging up a little piece of window; it would be *breaking* them. And it would be front-page headlines, if anyone knew.

"Does that mean you can, like, fly?" said Abby. She turned on the bench seat, folding one leg under her to face Eliza more comfortably.

"I get off the ground, okay?"

"But what's your trigger?" said Ricky, pestering her. "Tell more! Come on. I told you mine!"

Eliza just stared out the window some more. She was not, Abby had decided, a warm and fuzzy person.

"Fair's fair," Abby said, feeling a little bit pushy but also desperately curious.

"It's not a big deal," Eliza said, but she was starting to feel outvoted.

"Flying is a very big deal, Eliza," Ben chimed in.

"It's not flying! I didn't say flying," Eliza said, finally turning to face the others. "Did I say flying? I did not."

"You said levitation. That means rising off the ground," Ben said. "How is that not flying?"

"Because—well, because it's—"

Eliza stopped and looked down at her lap.

"Because it's what?" asked Abby, as gently as she could.

"Because I can only levitate a quarter of an inch."

There was a moment of shocked silence, and then came dual snorts from the back seat, as the boys looked at each other with raised eyebrows and tried to stifle their laughter. Abby also felt like giggling—what was the point of being able to fly, if you could only rise the height of an Oreo?—but she didn't want Eliza to regret having opened up.

"That's very cool," she told Eliza encouragingly. "Actually it's amazing." A little white lie never hurt anyone.

"It's not," Eliza retorted. "It's totally stupid. I've never even told anyone."

"You must have told *someone*," Ricky pointed out. "Or you wouldn't be here."

"Like Ferd?" said Abby. She couldn't help noticing that everybody's favorite weirdo seemed to play a central part in getting everybody on this van.

"I didn't exactly tell him," Eliza replied. "My counselor told him. She caught me."

The others were all completely rapt with attention, eyes wide. Eliza sighed. She'd have to spill her guts now.

"Okay, look. It's a totally lame power, okay? I can only levitate a tiny bit. And even then, I can't keep my balance. It's like if you were trying to balance on a bunch of marbles on the ground. You'd slip and slide all over the place. That's what it's like. It's totally useless."

"Why can't you just hold on to something?" asked Ricky.

"Well, I do. I have to, or else I'll fall right over."

Using both hands, Eliza flicked her cloud of orange hair off her shoulders, a habit she had whenever she was a little nervous. She plucked at the folds of her enormous T-shirt to adjust it a little.

128

"So how did someone see you using your power?" asked Ben.

"Okay, well, one night I was trying to sneak out of my bunk in Witches 2 to get a snack from the fridge. Normally, nobody ever gets out of bed after lights out, because you can hear the footsteps. The floor, like, creaks. But it's no big deal for me because I'm not actually *touching* the floor. I sort of hover just above it, as long as I'm holding on to the bunk beds for balance. I sort of scooch myself along by pushing off the posts of the beds and stuff. Like I'm on a really, really flat skateboard."

Abby felt just a tiny bit cheated. *That,* she thought, *almost doesn't even count as levitation.*

"It was great because I didn't make any sound. I got all the way over to the mini-fridge without ever touching the ground. We had just made s'mores that night, and there were some leftover chocolate bars in the fridge. I stole one and grabbed a couple graham crackers, and not a soul knew it!"

She was warming up now, pleased with herself.

"So how'd you get caught?" Abby asked.

"What's a s'more?" said Ricky.

Eliza answered Ricky first. "You know, where you roast a marshmallow on a stick and then mush it between two graham crackers with a piece of a chocolate bar, so it gets all melted and gooey. It's awesome!"

Eliza lived in New York City, where very few people made campfires in the summer. So to her, s'mores were a huge discovery.

"How'd you get caught?" Ben asked.

"Oh," said Eliza, losing some of her enthusiasm. "I was trying to float back to my bunk, but it was too hard to carry the food in one hand and keep myself steady with the other one. So I wound up losing my balance and falling on my butt. I tried to get up and levitate again, back to my bunk, but when I hit the floor, I woke up my counselor. I didn't know it at the time, but she was watching me go the whole way back."

She shrugged. "Next morning, I had a visit from Ferd at breakfast. Right, Ferd?"

But he didn't reply. He was either lost in iPod Land again or pretending to be.

"Anyway. Here I am." She didn't seem too happy about it. Then again, Eliza never seemed too happy about anything.

"What's your trigger?" said Ricky, who was much more easily fired up. "What makes it happen? What do you have to do?"

Eliza made it clear that she didn't want to discuss her trigger. "That's my little secret," is all she said.

"Why, Eliza? Why don't you want to tell us?" asked Abby.

"We're your friends here," added Ben. "Whatever it is, we're not going to judge you." He was hoping she'd forgotten the little giggle-snort he'd made when he found out her power.

Eliza looked out the window at the passing landscape, which had given way to a greener world of rolling hills.

"Doesn't matter," Eliza said. "It's not something I want to talk about, okay? Let it drop."

"Well, I know it's not something you *say*, like my trigger is," Ricky piped up. "Because then they would have heard you in the cabin that night."

"And it's not something you *do* with your hands, like my trigger," Abby added, enjoying the game. "Because you needed your hands to hold on to the bunk beds so you wouldn't fall over."

"Okay, fine!" said Eliza, finally, rolling her eyes. "Okay. It's not something I say, and it's not something with my hands. It's something I *think*."

"Coooooool!" Ricky exclaimed. "You can do it just by thinking?"

"Yes," Eliza said. "I think about a herd of buffalos. Satisfied?"

"Well, what's so embarrassing about that?" asked Abby. "You acted like it was something that people would make fun of."

"Well, it's not just buffalos. I have to think about buffalos that . . . are all walking backward."

"A herd of buffalos walking backward?" said Ben. "Man, that's pretty specific."

"Yeah," muttered Eliza. "A herd of buffalos walking backward and wearing . . ."

"Wearing what?" said Ricky.

"Is this the embarrassing part?" asked Abby.

"Yeah."

"Oooooh, let's guess!" shouted Ricky. "I bet it's, like, ballerina tutus! Is it tutus?"

"No, no, nothing like that."

"Regular clothes? Is it some kind of regular clothes?" offered Ben.

"No!"

"It's got to be something more embarrassing than that, or she would have told us," Abby pointed out. "Is it, like, underpants?"

"No! Not exactly," muttered Eliza.

"A bib?" offered Ben.

"Is it a *bra?*" blurted Ricky, giggling hysterically.

Eliza glared at him. "No, no, no!" she said. "Nothing like that." She stared miserably ahead at the dashboard. It was half a minute before she spoke again.

"The buffalos have to be wearing diapers. Happy now?"

The three other kids, having promised not to laugh, did everything they could to contain themselves.

"Ohhhhh," said Ricky solemnly, but the "ohhh" soon fell apart into a paroxysm of coughing that was designed to mask his giggling. Abby, trying desperately to conceal her huge grin, covered her face with her arm as she pretended to scratch her opposite ear.

Ben tried to think sad thoughts, tried to focus on the scenery, tried to hold his breath—but he couldn't hold it. A weird sort of noise exploded out of him, sort of a cross between a laugh and a loud burp.

Eliza glared at him.

"Sorry," he muttered.

"Okay, so . . ." Ricky was biting the sides of his tongue, hoping that the pain would stop him from laughing about a herd of backward-walking buffalos wearing diapers. He cleared his throat loudly several times, but his stomach was tense and quivering with the suppressed laughter.

Abby, who had managed to pull herself together, tried to change the subject, at least slightly. "That's really amazing, Eliza. Seriously. How did you ever discover your power?"

Eliza sighed. "It was a TV show called *The Ren and Stimpy Show*, this really, really old cartoon from a long time ago. My parents had it on a videotape. Sometimes they'd put on these tapes for my brother and me when they wanted to get us out of their hair for a while.

"Anyway, they put this one tape in the VCR, and we watched it, and there was a part with these baby buffalos, and they were all wearing diapers. It was pretty funny, actually."

"But they were walking backward?"

"No, no, they were walking normally," Eliza responded. "But my brother wanted to go back and show me his favorite part again. So he was rewinding the VCR, you know, scanning backward, and that makes it play in reverse. So it looked like all these buffalos in diapers were walking backward. And suddenly I just—I just floated up off the couch. Just a little tiny bit. But it felt *so* freaky, and it was so unexpected, that I, like, screamed a little. And my brother's like, 'Cut it out, Lize.' And I'm like, 'I can't help it! Did you see that?' And he's like, 'What?' And so I realized that it happened to me, but not to him. So I didn't want him to know. So I said, 'That buffalo part. I love that.' He had barely even noticed it."

Abby was surprised that Eliza was talking so much. Until this moment, she hadn't heard Eliza say more than a couple sentences at a time.

"Anyway, now my brother starts scanning *forward*, to get to the buffalo scene again. And I sank back into the couch.

And he hits Play and he's like, 'What, this part?' And I'm like, 'Yeah—isn't that hilarious?' And he goes, 'Whatever.' And he hits Rewind again. So now the buffalos are all walking backward again, and I'm thinking about it again, and up I go!

"So I'm a little freaked out, so I go upstairs to my room. But on the stairs, I'm thinking about what just happened. And I'm remembering that it only happened when my brother was rewinding through that one scene. And every time I thought about that scene, it would happen *again*! I actually levitated right there on the stairs. I mean, you know. A tiny bit. But I lost my balance. I almost fell over and cracked my head open!"

It was about the most bizarre story Abby had ever, ever heard.

"So you never told anyone?"

Eliza shook her head. "Practically nobody." And she left it at that.

"Hey," Ben said. "Can we—can we see? I mean, can you show us?" He shot a glance at Abby for support.

"Forget it," snapped Eliza. "I don't do it on command. I'm not a trained dog."

"Aw, come on," said Ricky. "I showed you mine!"

"And I'll show you mine as soon as we get, you know, some eggs," added Abby.

"That's a No." Eliza was firm. "It's not gonna happen."

But Ben had a twinkle in his eye. "So your trigger is just picturing—you know, that one particular image of that certain animal dressed—that certain way?"

"Yes! I told you."

"And every time you think of it, you levitate?"

"Yes. What's your point?"

"So to make you levitate, all we'd have to do is get you to think about that certain subject?"

Eliza turned to face him. "Yes, but you can't. I'm too good. I've learned to think about other things."

Ben held up a notebook, open to a page.

"Even if I showed you this?"

You couldn't *really* tell whether his drawing showed buffalos, cows, hamsters, or what; Ben was a terrible artist. But it was clear that whatever they were, they had something diaper-ish wrapped around their hind legs. And he'd drawn a huge 3-D arrow pointing away from them, as though to suggest that they were walking backward.

Let's put it this way: if you'd just been talking for twenty minutes about buffalos walking backward, and now you were trying *not* to think about that, seeing Ben's drawing would definitely make you think about it again.

If you were watching closely, you could have seen

Eliza's entire body pop up. Not a lot—just enough to look as though she were a marionette whose strings had just been jerked a bit.

"Hey!" Eliza shouted, grabbing the seat in front of her for support.

"Abby! Here!" Ben tossed his notebook over the seat to her.

Abby knew right away what it was for. She smiled, grabbed the notebook, and slid it along the seat toward Eliza. And sure enough: it slid freely and easily under Eliza's rear end.

It was the easiest science project Abby had ever done.

"It's true, folks," she announced. "Nothing under Eliza right now but thin air."

It didn't take long for Eliza to start thinking about something else besides animals in potty training. In a blink, she sank right back down onto the seat, pinning the notebook under her.

She glared around the van. "That was not cool," she seethed. She yanked Ben's notebook out from under her and angrily threw it at him. It hit him in the forehead.

Abby didn't like Eliza much, but she didn't feel good about making her upset, either.

"I'm sorry, Eliza," she said sincerely. "We shouldn't have done that."

Ben rubbed his forehead and put his slightly mushed notebook back in his backpack. "Me, too. Sorry."

"It's kinda neat, though," said Ricky enthusiastically. (There was almost nothing Ricky ever said that *didn't* sound enthusiastic.) "You can do your power just by thinking about it."

"And it's a great power, too," said Abby encouragingly. "It's a lot more useful than spinning an egg."

"Or fogging up glass," added Ricky.

"Or flipping a key," Ben pointed out.

This last point seemed to interest Eliza.

"What do you mean, flipping a key?" she said, calming down at last.

"Is that your power?" asked Ricky. "Can I see?"

Abby looked back at Ben, alarmed. She was under the impression that Ben did not, in fact, have any special power at all. In fact, she had absolutely no idea what he was doing in the van.

CHAPTER
14
Sushi

"**B**EN. *WHAT ARE YOU DOING HERE?*"

Abby had managed to keep her mouth shut for what had seemed like two years in that van. She was smart enough to recognize that Ben was up to something—and to keep her own mouth shut. But she couldn't wait to talk to him in private.

She finally got her chance. Ferd had spotted a Sushi Shack, his favorite fast-food restaurant, just off the highway, and announced that it was definitely time for dinner. For two reasons: first, Ferd was hungry.

Second, Ricky was getting carsick.

But it wasn't until they had slid into the plastic booths in the Sushi Shack and placed their orders that Abby finally saw her opportunity. Ben got up to visit the men's room, so Abby excused herself and left the table at the same time.

She cornered Ben right by the goldfish tanks on his way back from the bathroom and whispered as loudly as she dared.

"Ben. *What are you doing here?*"

He pretended not to know what she meant. "Well, I was sort of hoping to enjoy some slabs of raw fish."

"Come on! You know what I mean. Why are you part of this group? Ricky and Eliza and I all have these—these dumb little powers. But you . . . you told me that you don't! You said you're just a magician! You said you didn't even believe that there's . . . you know, real magic, or whatever."

Ben leaned back against the glass of the aquarium. "What can I say? I lied."

"You lied? What do you mean? To me?"

"No, not to you. To Ferd."

Abby was shocked. "You mean, he thinks your key trick is an actual power?"

"Hey—it fooled you, remember?" Ben wiggled his eyebrows. "After I heard about your invitation to super camp, I kind of showed off my key trick to a kid at lunch at the same table where Ferd was eating. He took me aside afterward

140

and asked me if I'd share how I did it. And so I said what I always said."

"That even you don't know how you do it."

Ben nodded. "Yep. Once you'd told me about getting invited to the super camp, I kind of knew what to say already. I knew what Ferd was going to suggest."

"But why? I mean, why did you want to come?"

"Are you kidding? 'Cuz it's fun! See the world a little! Get out of camp for a little while. Hang out with you. You know, find out what happens at the camp for magician freaks." He looked very pleased with himself.

Abby still wasn't comfortable with the whole thing. "But what if you get caught?" she asked.

"What if I do?" He shrugged. "They'll send me back to camp, I guess. What else can they do?"

Abby couldn't believe that he'd do anything so risky. She looked down at the floor.

"They're probably gonna find out, Ben."

Ben shrugged. "So what? It'll be fun while it lasts. Let's see how long we can stay on this ride. You're not gonna tell, are you?"

She shook her head no.

"Okay, then. We're partners with a secret, right? Come on, let's go back to the table. My California rolls are getting cold."

They made their way back to the table and rejoined the others. Everyone was eating sushi except Eliza, who said she was allergic.

("To fish?" Ricky had said.

"No, to rice." She had a hot dog instead.)

Ferd had just piled a chunk of wasabi onto his tuna roll and was preparing to slam the whole thing into his mouth when Abby and Ben returned.

"Aha, they're back," he said. "We were just talking about you."

"Oh, yeah?" Ben said, sitting down. "Only nice things, I'm sure."

"Everyone's told their stories except you," Eliza said accusingly. "You practically haven't said a word since we crossed the New York state line."

Ben smiled. "I'm a man of few words. What can I say?"

"I wanna see his power," said Ricky. There was a single grain of white rice stuck to his cheek, which bobbed up and down whenever he spoke.

"I don't know. It's kind of dumb," Ben said modestly.

"It's not dumb," said Abby encouragingly. "Just show 'em."

Eliza shot her a suspicious look. "You've seen it?"

Abby nodded. "I met Ben the first day of camp."

"Okay, then, let's see your trick. You've already seen *mine*," she added dryly.

Ben fished in his pocket for the car key he always used. He held out his flat palm. "Can everyone see okay?"

Everyone could.

He put the key flat on his hand and said the words Abby had heard before. "I'm not going to touch this key. I'm not going to blow on it. No strings attached. All it is . . . is a momentary flux of gravity."

And he squeezed one eye shut. Ricky gave a little gasp as the key slowly, visibly lifted up on its edge and then fell over on its back.

"Wow, that is *wicked*," breathed Ricky. "You could use that as a real magic trick, you know? It's not like our powers, like, totally pointless. That one, you could do in a show."

"I do, actually," said Ben. "I've been doing magic shows since I was nine. I do a lot of birthday parties."

Eliza was studying him carefully. "So you were into magic *before* you discovered you had a power?"

"No, not really," Ben replied. "I've been able to move the key like that since I was about seven years old."

Abby noticed how he was choosing his words carefully. Clearly, Ben didn't want to just come right out and lie, yet he did want the others to keep thinking that his power was real.

"And what's your trigger, exactly?" asked Eliza, probing.

"It's that thing with your eye, right?" asked Ricky, proud of himself for noticing. "When you squint your eye, that's what makes it turn over."

Ben smiled, but Abby sensed that he was getting uncomfortable with his game of pretending. She stepped in to help.

"Yeah, exactly," she said, nominating herself to be his official spokesperson. "Ben, you probably have the least weird trigger of anyone here."

"Yeah, maybe," he answered with a grateful half smile.

"From whence do you hail, Ben?" chimed in Ferd.

Ben looked at him blankly. Ferd rolled his eyes and then asked a different way: "Where are you from?"

"New Jersey," he said. "But we've moved around a lot for my dad's job."

Abby suddenly realized that she didn't know much about Ben's background at all. "Do you have any brothers or sisters?" she asked.

"Nope," he replied. "Only child."

"Are you gonna be a magician when you grow up?" asked Ricky. He was obviously impressed that Ben was already doing magic shows for money.

"I don't know," Ben said. "I like it. I like performing magic, I like watching it, I even like teaching it. I taught beginning magic to little kids at a summer camp near my house last year. But my parents keep telling me it's too hard to earn money doing magic."

"Hmph," Ferd chimed in. "I would advise you not to mention that to David Copperfield, or Lance Burton, or Criss Angel, or David Blaine."

Abby grinned. Ferd was a hardcore magic nerd.

"How'd you get picked to go to super camp?" Eliza asked, still sounding a little skeptical of Ben's story.

"Let me guess: Ferd," offered Abby.

"You are correct, young lady," Ferd said. "I saw Mr. Wheeler performing his remarkable key effect in the dining hall one day."

"Yeah," said Ben, picking up the story. "He asked me how it works, and I told him I didn't know. Next thing I knew, he asked if I wanted to meet other kids with— unusual abilities, so I said sure! I'm always up for an adventure."

"Oh, you'll have one of those, all right." Ferd nodded, his greasy ponytail bobbing. "And it's going to start soon. We're only about one more hour away."

The kids had long since stopped studying the view out the window. If they had paid more attention, they would have noticed the gradual, slow alternation of cities, suburbs, and countryside—and they would have noticed that for the last hour, it had been all countryside, and even a couple of cornfields.

Night was falling when the van finally slowed to a stop. The kids pressed their faces to the windows to see where they were.

They were at a magnificent, ten-foot, black wrought-iron gate in an impressive stone wall. Abby could see one end of a laser-engraved bronze sign mounted to the wall. The first two letters were CA; the rest of the name was covered by a cloth that some painter had left draped over the wall.

A security guard in a glass booth recognized Ferd, gave him a friendly wave, and pressed a button; the huge black gates swung open on electronic hinges to let the van through.

The view before them was stunning. They were at the top rim of a gently sloped valley, which was so big you couldn't see the whole thing without turning your head. The grass was brilliant green as far as the eye could see; the setting sun gave the entire scene a golden sheen.

Nestled at the bottom of the valley was what Abby first thought was a little village, or maybe a college campus—ten or twelve clean white buildings connected by walkways and decorated by artistically placed trees, plants, and flowers. In the center of the cluster of buildings was a lavishly gardened courtyard with a fountain that shot out what must have been a thirty-foot-tall spire of water.

The access road wound gently down the hill toward the little village, and Ferd drove slowly so they could appreciate the view. As they approached, Abby could see that it wasn't a village or even a college campus; the buildings looked a little too sleek and modern.

When she was a little girl, Abby's dad had once taken her to visit his airline's headquarters. She'd been very excited. She'd imagined that it would be like some huge *Star Wars* spaceship dock, a busy place where people were attaching wings onto airplanes, cooking airplane meals, watching huge screens that showed where all the planes in the air were—stuff like that. It had turned out to be nothing like that at all. The airline headquarters was just an office building—a plain, all-glass office mini-skyscraper, with carpeting, fluorescent lights, little cubicles, and hundreds of workers tapping away on computer keyboards. That was it. No wings, no meals, no giant screens.

That's how she felt when she saw the super camp for the first time. At first glance, it didn't actually look much like a camp at all. She didn't see any kids, any parents, any lake except for the fountain pond. There weren't even any activity areas—soccer fields, tennis courts, a pool, that sort of thing—at least not that she could see. It was beautiful, but it sure wasn't Camp Cadabra.

"Is that the super camp?" asked Ricky. *Bless his heart,* Abby thought. *He's having the same reaction I am.*

"Super-duper," replied Ferd.

Abby stole a look at Ben. He was staring hard out the window with a look of concern.

"It doesn't *look* like a camp," blurted Eliza.

"My dear, you're going to love it," was all Ferd said.

He pulled the van up to one of the closest buildings. It had a low-slung roof, and the entire front wall was made of glass, so you could see the sleek wood floors and shiny silver furniture of the lobby inside. A skinny blond man with a tidy little mustache was standing by the front door waiting for them. He was wearing a suit and tie, which Abby thought was a little odd for summer camp. He was also wearing a pair of glasses and a big smile.

Ferd climbed out and walked around the van to open the doors for Abby, Ben, Ricky, and Eliza.

"Come on out, my people," he said. "Welcome to your home away from home. You're gonna love it here."

From the looks of the place, Abby wasn't quite so sure.

CHAPTER
15
Orientation

THE GUY IN THE SUIT was super-friendly, and, Abby thought, also super-weird. He sure didn't act like the director of the camp. He acted more like their puppy.

"Greetings, greetings all!" he exclaimed. "We've been expecting you! So thrilled, so thrilled!"

He was a one-man welcoming committee. He rushed to grab each kid's hand and shook it like he was pumping water. "Hello there—Phil Shutter. How are you? I'm Phil— nice to meet you. Phil Shutter; I run this place. Great to see you, thanks for coming. Here, let me get that bag for you. No, no, please—call me Phil."

Abby and Ben happened to glance at each other at exactly the same moment. Clearly, they were both thinking the same thing. Which, if you had to put it into words, was something like: "*What the*—?!?!"

"So everybody survived? It must have been quite a ride," Phil was going on. As he spoke, he was trying to prop open the big glass front door with his heel while hauling duffel bags into the lobby. "I've made the drive many times myself; I know what you've been through! But you're in good hands with Ferd. Okay, watch the corner there— good girl."

Abby had never seen Phil before in her life, and yet she recognized his voice. It was weirdly familiar. A little bit singsongy, a little bit nasal—where had she heard that voice before?

Eventually, they all made it into the lobby. Phil finally stopped talking—at least to them. Instead, he began speaking to a pretty receptionist at the front desk. She made a quick phone call, and within seconds, three guys in matching black work shirts arrived to take the kids' duffel bags.

Phil invited them to plop down on the big leather chairs. He pulled one of them around so that he could sit on it and face them.

"Okle-dokle," he began, glancing down at his clipboard. "First, I want to welcome you to the Camp Cadabra advanced-placement program. It's really a big honor for me to meet you folks—I've been waiting for you a long time. You and the other kids."

Ricky shot his hand straight up like a lightning rod. "What other kids?"

Phil smiled. "Good question—Ben? Are you Ben? Oh, no—Ricky. Ricky. Well, as you may know, there's more than one Camp Cadabra. In fact, we've opened up summer camps for young magicians all around the country. Five of them in all. We like to think that they're the finest magic camps in America. And at each camp, we're looking for youngsters like you who have . . . *special* abilities. Something beyond plain old magic tricks; I think you all know what I mean. All four of you have come from our New Hampshire camp. But tonight at the social, you'll meet the kids we've invited from the other camps. It's a very special group. Very, very, very, *very* special." His glasses had slipped down on his nose; he took this moment to push them back up with one finger and peer at the kids through them.

"Now, I know you've probably got a lot of questions, so I want you all to think of me as your answer man. I'm absolutely full of answers! I'd better be—I run this place!" He paused and looked eagerly from face to face, hoping for laughter. There wasn't any.

"In the meantime," he went on, "Ferd will be staying

with you at this facility, so he'll always be on hand if you need anything in particular. But for now, I know you're all probably very tired after that long ride. Why don't we show you to the guest rooms, and then we'll all meet in the restaurant for a bedtime snack in half an hour?"

Guest rooms? Restaurant? It was starting to sound more like a hotel than a summer camp.

Phil stood up, pushed his chair back where it had come from, and motioned for them to follow. "Okay—enough chit-chat. Come-come! I can't wait for you to see the place."

"Hey!" shouted Eliza as she stood up. She'd been quiet quite long enough, and now the brassy New Yorker in her was bubbling to the surface. "How come there's no lake or cabins or anything? What kind of camp is this?"

But Phil was already walking briskly away. "It's a wonderful place, wonderful. We built it just for you! You're going to love it."

Ben wasn't quite getting it, either. He trotted to catch up. "Well, if there are only a few kids here, how come there are so many buildings?"

Phil didn't even bother to look back at him; he kept right on striding along. "Running a chain of camps all across the country is a big project," he replied with a shrug. "Gotta have headquarters somewhere, right?"

As he took them out the back of the lobby and into a long, carpeted hallway, the group thinned out to fit the narrower space. Abby was getting squished against a wall. "Excuse me! Mr. Shutter?"

"Phil! Call me Phil. Always Phil, okay? That's how we roll here." He gave her a wink. Or tried to; Phil couldn't actually wink, so he wound up blinking both eyes at her and just looking really strange.

"Okay, Phil?" Abby said, trotting to keep up. "Can I call my parents? I haven't talked to them in, like, forever."

"There'll be plenty of time for that," Phil replied. "In the meantime, there's a brand-new laptop right in every guest room, so feel free to drop them an e-mail or what have you."

Hmmmph! Abby thought. *For a guy who says he's here to give us answers, he sure doesn't have a lot of them.*

They rounded a corner and came to a doorway. Next to it was a small black box. Phil unclipped a little plastic security card from his belt and waved it in front of the box; instantly, a little green light turned on, and the door unlocked with a loud click.

"My dad has that at his bank where he works," Eliza said to nobody in particular. "It's for security."

"You are quite correct, little lady," Phil replied. "Your parents have entrusted you to our care, and so your safety is our

153

absolute priority. Nobody gets into the camper area without one of these security cards. In fact, after hours, we turn on motion detectors in this hallway, and even pressure sensors in the floor. You may find that excessive, but hey: you folks are special, and we intend to keep you safe and sound. You never know who *else* might think you're special. We don't want anyone coming in here except the good guys."

He made another attempt at winking, but just wound up looking like he'd gotten dust in his eyes.

They made their way through yet another vestibule into yet another lobby with yet another receptionist sitting at yet another front desk. "This is Candi," Phil said. "You four are staying right here in this pod, and she'll be on duty right here at the desk if you need anything at all."

Candi handed Phil a set of four card keys, which he handed out to the four kids.

"Annnnnnnd, here we are," Phil finally announced, sweeping his arm. "Find your place!"

The "pod," as Phil called it, consisted of four rooms, all connecting to Candi's little lobby. One camper's name appeared on a little plaque next to each door.

Abby walked up to hers, but before she slid her key card into it, she took a cautious look back at Ben. He was already at his own door across the lobby, trying to figure out which way to slide his key into the slot.

She turned back to her own door, swiped her key card, and stepped inside.

It wasn't a camp cabin, that's for sure. It was—well, it looked like a really, really expensive hotel room. The bed was big enough for six people to sleep on. Enormous glass picture windows formed the back wall, with a view out to the courtyard and the gigantic fountain. Next to the head-board of the bed, Abby found a panel full of buttons that you could push without even getting up. One of these buttons opened and closed the curtains. Another one turned off all the lights in the room.

The first time Abby pressed the third button, she just about jumped out of her skin. An electronic whirring noise started coming from the bureau opposite the bed—and then, from a hidden slot, up came a flat-panel TV the size of Kansas. It rose up as though it were riding an invisible elevator.

"Whooooooaaa," she said out loud.

There was a super-thin, shiny new laptop on the desk, and an iPod in a mini-stereo, and a leather desk chair that had a remote control of its own; not only could it adjust in about sixty-four different ways, but it could also massage your back. That degree of overkill, Abby soon learned, was just about everywhere—like in the bathroom, which had a hot tub, a regular bathtub, and a shower. And the shower had, no kidding, *eight* different sprayers, to make sure there wasn't one single inch of your body that didn't get squirted. She wanted to call over to Ben's room, so they could say "Whooooooooaaaa" together.

But even though her room had more high-tech gadgetry than the space shuttle, she was surprised to find one obvious item missing: there was no phone.

CHAPTER
16
Social

IN ALL OF HER TV INTERVIEWS, Abby seems to remember a million details of her adventure at the super camp. But the part she remembers best is the meet-and-greet social—the party to welcome everybody to the super camp.

It was outdoors in the courtyard, the one with the huge fountain. Phil Shutter had ordered the whole place to be decorated with these eight-foot-tall torches, accompanied by good music, and outfitted with huge tables of kid-friendly food. The sun was setting, filling the whole place with a golden light, and the air was just warm enough that you could wear a short-sleeved shirt.

Abby, who had once felt so alone with her weird useless power, was amazed to find out that there were, in fact, twenty-three kids here—teenagers, middle-schoolers, even a couple of elementary-schoolers. And every one of them had some pointless special power that they'd never asked for.

It didn't take long for Abby to find Ben, Ricky, and Eliza. They were hanging out by the fountain, munching chocolate-covered nuts that they had sneaked from a bowl on a table. And it wasn't long after that when she realized that *all* of the kids were hanging out in clusters—according to the camps they'd come from. You'd be amazed at how quickly you can bond with other kids when you spend nine hours with them in a van.

Or on a plane. Some of the other kids had come from Cadabra camps as far away as California.

"Hey there, ho there!"

Abby looked up to see that Phil Shutter had stepped into the light with a microphone.

"Could we dial that music down a bit? Thank you ever so kindly!"

He pushed his glasses up his nose. For the big party, Abby noticed, he had taken off his tie. He no longer looked like a businessman at a summer camp; now he looked like a businessman with his tie off.

"Greetings to you all," he began, as corny as ever. Abby and Ben exchanged eye-rolling glances.

"It's good to see all of you folks together in one place. I hope you've all had a chance to settle in, get your stuff unpacked, and learn how the shower works. If you have any questions at all, please let me know, or just tell the receptionist in your pod lobby, and she'll get whatever you need."

Kermit the Frog! That's who Phil sounded exactly like— Kermit the Frog.

"He sounds like Kermit!" Abby whispered directly into Ben's ear. He listened for a moment, and then nodded, grinning, as he recognized the voice, too.

"Anyhoo," Phil was going on, "tonight it's all about meeting your camp mates and your new counselors, enjoying a little delicious barbeque, and recovering from your journey. Tomorrow, the work begins. Whoops! Did I say work? I meant fun! Because around here, work is fun. I expect you'll really enjoy meeting our staff tomorrow. They'll work with you to help you understand your power, to make it grow, to help you use it in better ways."

He scratched at his little mustache with the end of his pen and glanced around the courtyard.

"Okeydoke," he said. "Now, in just a moment, we'll bring out a little grub. Grab a plastic plate and fill it up, *hombres!* And then I want to give each of you an assignment. I want you to walk right up to somebody you don't know, somebody from a different Cadabra camp, and introduce yourself. Tell a little about yourself. Say where you're from, what grade you're in. If you're comfortable with it, do a little show-and-tell of your power. I wanna see some serious mingling. Let's get this party started!"

Unfortunately, Phil was trying to say it the way a rock star would say it, so it came out like, "Let's get this potty stotted!"

Ben nudged Abby with his elbow. "Oh, he's a cool one, that Phil," he said, shaking his head.

She laughed. "Come on—let's pig out."

So they filled their plastic plates with chicken, ribs, salad, mashed potatoes, corn, and brownies. At first, Abby and Ben sat on the little wall around the fountain, ate, and chatted; but after a while, they decided that Phil's suggestion was worth taking. This was a great opportunity to meet the other campers and find out their stories.

As it turned out, there were some interesting stories indeed.

A tall, black-haired girl named Doreen had been dumped at Camp Cadabra in Indiana by her parents, who were in the middle of a divorce and didn't want her hanging around the house all summer. She had zero interest in magic except for her own power, which was raising her body temperature by two degrees.

She had occasionally been able to use it to get out of going to school ("Mom, I feel sick! I think I have a fever!"), but otherwise thought it was no more useful than, say, having a freckle on her arm.

"What's your trigger?" Ben asked.

"My what?" Evidently, not every Camp Cadabra had a Ferd to explain what triggers are.

"How do you make your body temperature go up?"

"Oh. Like this."

Doreen lifted her arms out to her sides, waving them and sticking her stomach this way and that. Abby wasn't exactly sure what she was doing, apart from looking a little like a tippy scarecrow.

But Ben caught on. "Belly dancing! You're belly dancing, right?"

Doreen nodded. "Now feel!" She grabbed Ben's hand and pulled it up to her own forehead. Ben was no doctor, but her forehead did feel a little warm.

"And that's not just from the exercise of dancing around?" Abby asked.

"Nope," said Doreen. "That's what everybody asks. I stay hot for, like, two hours. And you can measure it with a thermometer."

They also met a tall, gangly, weed-thin kid going into high school who called himself Weezer. (Months later, after the whole story came out in the newspapers, they learned that Weezer's real name was Eugene.)

He had flown all the way in from the California camp because his counselors had discovered his amazing ability— to clog a salt shaker.

"Salt shakers git clogged all the time," he explained in a slow, booming voice with a twangy Southern accent. "Usually it's because of humidity, like in the summertime when it's hot and muggy out. But I can do better'n that. I can clog it when I want to clog it. I can clog it even when it ain't cloggy weather."

Abby nodded appreciatively. She congratulated Weezer because he seemed genuinely proud of his talent. And why not? It was something that nobody else could do. She even managed to avoid smiling when she learned about his trigger: crossing his toes. Even if it was inside his shoes, it still worked. You could even be right in the middle of shaking out salt onto your food; if Weezer crossed his toes, that was it. No more salt. You'd have to get a toothpick and poke it into the little holes to un-jam them.

Then there was Tabor, who was standing by the brownie tray when Abby and Ben went for seconds. Tabor was visiting from Hungary. He had been staying with an American host family in Florida who had a son the same age. The son, named Eric, had always been a magic nut, sitting in his room and practicing card moves or coin tricks for hours; he had been begging his parents all winter and spring for the chance to go to magic camp. He was sure it would be the greatest thing in the world.

Tabor's life was filled with magic, too, but not in the same way. He had never even thought about magic as a form of entertainment. His family believed in all kinds of mystical things; his mother used to say they had Gypsy blood in them. Growing up, he'd heard stories of distant relatives who could read minds, or bring rain to dry fields, or miraculously cure sickness. Nobody could ever prove it, of course, and nobody had ever actually seen any of it. But from the time he was a baby, Tabor had been taught that miracles, large and small, are woven into the cloth of everyday life.

Tabor believed that if you dig deep enough, you'll find something magical, or at least unusual, in everybody. His uncle Viktor could stick out his tongue and make the sides crinkle up with wavy edges. A kid in his school could roll his eyes so far back in his head, all you could see was pure white, like a zombie. And his cousin Kristina could breathe through her ear. For real. (The doctor said there was some kind of connection between her ear canal and her nasal cavity.)

And Tabor himself was double-jointed. That's what

you call people who can bend their joints much farther than normal people. Tabor showed Abby how, using his other hand, he could bend his thumb back so far that it could touch his wrist. (Even today, Abby can't get her own thumb anywhere near her wrist. Plus, it hurts to try.)

One day, when he was about eight years old, Tabor was showing off his thumb-bending thing to a friend. All of a sudden, a piece of mail fell off his father's desk.

And that was how he discovered his power. It turns out that if you put a sheet of paper at the edge of a desk or a table so that half of it is sticking out, *almost* falling off the edge, he can make it fall. It's as though he can make gravity just the *tiniest* bit stronger on the suspended half of the sheet of paper, just enough to tip it off the table.

Tabor didn't think it was a big deal. Growing up in Hungary, he just accepted it as another one of life's freaky little unexplained oddities.

But Eric, the boy his age in the American host family, went crazy. When he saw Tabor knock the sheet of paper off the desk without touching it, he thought it was the greatest magic trick he'd ever seen.

Eric begged Tabor to teach him how to do it. Tabor explained that he didn't know how it worked, but Eric didn't believe him. He just believed that Tabor was sticking to the old magician's rule, "Never reveal your secrets." And that's how it came about that Eric and Tabor *both* went to the Camp Cadabra in Georgia that summer. Eric wanted to become a better entertainer; Tabor just wanted to see more of America. The twist, of course, is that Tabor, who had very little interest in magic as a form of entertainment, got chosen to come to the super camp. And Eric, his own American "brother," the one *real* magician among them, didn't. He stayed behind at Camp Cadabra.

As the evening went on, more of the campers shared their stories. Some accepted their powers, just the way you might accept having brown hair or bony elbows. But many of them had been suffering in silence, feeling like weirdos, getting teased at school, getting no understanding from their parents, brothers, and sisters.

And yet here, under a sky full of summer stars, they were among friends. Nobody would laugh at you; if there was a smile when you were telling about your embarrassing little power, it was a smile of understanding and sympathy. Here, you could talk about your magic, your secret, your journey so far.

There was also a lot of talk about what would happen tomorrow, when super camp would finally begin for real.

Sent: June 30
From: acarnelia11@gmail.com
To: eastportmama@optonline.net
Subject: Howdy

Hey you guys,

Hey from your favorite daughter at super camp!

They just had a super-fun welcome party for all of
us kids. There's about 25 of us from all over the
country. They're all super-talented and really nice.
They had a big cookout, and we all had a lot of
fun.

The place is not much like a camp. It's beautiful,
though. The room is like a hotel room! Big plasma
TV, hot tub, and all that. There are three other
kids here from the camp I was at, including that
guy Ben, who I think you met the first day.

It's not at all what I expected. It's nothing like
a camp at all. It's like, I don't know, a big

modern company headquarters. But whatever.
Looks like fun.

How's everything with you guys? Does Ryan still
have his frog?

I'm super-tired, so I'm going to sleep now . . .
I'll e-mail some more tomorrow!

Love,
Abs

CHAPTER
17
Lab

ABBY DIDN'T SLEEP WELL her first night at super camp. She never slept well in new places. Her pillow at home was super-hyper-ultra-mushy, so whenever she had to use a pillow that was sort of hard and tall, she couldn't get comfortable. That night, though, things were even worse because it seemed as though she had nonstop nightmares.

In the worst and last one, she dreamed that she was running around outside, under a big sky, on a huge field, with a herd of wild horses. They were all romping, playing, happy to just be alive and free, and happy that Abby was among them.

But then Abby looked up at that glorious blue sky, and she noticed something odd: a reflection that shouldn't have been there. It was as though she were looking out through an infinite piece of curved glass. And sure enough, when she looked around, she realized that there was a gigantic glass dome, a huge transparent bubble that was slowly sinking down around the entire field.

She tried to scream, to tell all the horses that they would be trapped, but they couldn't understand her (they were horses, after all). So she ran around them, trying to shoo them away, as the glass dome sank lower and lower. It also started getting smaller and smaller, trapping them all inside.

Now she started yelling out to whoever was controlling the dome. "I'm not a horse! I'm not a horse! I'm a person! Let me go! Let me go!"

But there was no answer . . . and when she looked down at herself, she realized that it wasn't even true. She was a horse, too.

That's when she woke up, breathing hard and feeling desperate and sad.

She pressed her palms into her eyes and rubbed them. "Just a dream, just a dream, just a dream," she said to herself. She checked the clock; breakfast was only half an hour away, so it was time to get up and get the ball rolling.

The dining hall at this camp, she discovered, wasn't a dining hall—not even a super-fancy, ultra-cushy one like at Camp Cadabra. Instead, it was a straight-ahead cafeteria, just like the one at school except with better food and no fourth graders' artwork on the walls. It was a pretty big one, bigger than her school cafeteria, but almost everyone there was an adult. The kids all sat at a group of tables at one end of the room, where Ferd and four other helpers took charge.

"We commence at nine, so finish up," he said. Abby was sitting with Ricky and Eliza, who were both yawning; they'd stayed up even later than she had at the welcome party. Ricky was hyper, chattering nonstop. Eliza, wearing another T-shirt the size of Louisiana, ate silently.

Ben didn't show up at all.

After breakfast, everybody handed their trays through an opening in the wall to a dishwashing crew on the other side.

"Okay, let's go, my people," Ferd said. "New Hampshire campers, I'll take you to your first activity."

Funny, Abby thought. *I don't remember signing up for activities.*

Ferd led Abby, Ricky, and Eliza out of the cafeteria and through two long hallways; at the end of the second one, they found Ben waiting with Candi, the pod assistant.

"Looks like you've got yourself a troublemaker," she said with a smile. "I found this guy stumbling out of his room about ten minutes ago."

"I overslept," Ben said sheepishly.

"Thank you, Candi," replied Ferd. "Ben, would you care for a Pop-Tart or something?"

"I already got him a bagel," said Candi.

"I'm good," Ben confirmed.

"All right then—onward to Magic Central!"

Ferd swiped his security card across the little black box by a big set of heavy double doors. They swung open, Ferd plowed ahead, and the four kids scampered to keep up.

They were marching down a long, wide, white hallway. There were doors on both sides—doors with windows so you could see inside. Other kids, led by other camp workers, were flooding into the hallway and going into different doors. It felt like the first day of a new school.

As she marched along, Abby noticed that there was a small sign next to each door that identified what was going on inside—and they blew her mind.

METAMORPHOSIS. ESP. RESTORATION. TELEPORTATION. PREDICTION. DISAPPEARANCE. INVISIBILITY. BODY MORPH.

What is this place? Abby thought to herself. *Have they really found kids who can do all this stuff?*

Ferd stopped suddenly, and Abby almost crashed into Ricky.

"Eliza, m'dear, this is you," Ferd said. "I'll be back to pick you up at lunchtime."

The door looked just like all the others, except that it said LEVITATION. *Well, naturally,* thought Abby.

"See you, dudes," said Eliza with a shrug. She went inside.

Ferd moved forward about twenty feet to stop at the very next door. "Ricky, this would be you."

Ricky read the sign on the door out loud. "WEATHER PHENOMENA?" he said.

Ferd shrugged. "Well, we couldn't figure out how fogging up a window really fit into Levitation or Invisibility. Okay, young man, in you go. I'll see you at noon."

Ricky stayed right where he was in the hallway. He looked around with an unhappy face. "But can't I stay with my friends?"

"You'll see them at lunch," Ferd reassured him. "Go on inside. They won't bite. Trust me—fun and pleasure await." He pulled the door open for Ricky, who looked inside, looked back at Abby and Ben, and then muttered, "Well, okay, I'll see you guys." He turned and went inside.

Ferd let the door close gently, then turned to Ben and Abby. "And you youngsters are right over here."

He marched them to the end of the hallway and stopped in front of a door labeled TELEKINESIS.

"What's that?" asked Abby. "Tele-kine-sis? It sounds like a disease."

"No, it's cool," Ben reassured her. "It's called telekin-ee-sis. Moving things with your mind."

"And that's pretty much your specialty, no?" said Ferd. He opened the door for them. "This is you. Have a blast."

Abby stood in the doorway, peering into the room. It looked like a science fair, a kitchen, a magic shop, and somebody's basement playroom, all in one.

She could see broad tables surrounded by stools. Black-boards and whiteboards on the walls. Video cameras in all four corners of the ceiling. Sinks and cabinets everywhere. Cardboard boxes and plastic milk crates full of stuff. Tripods holding cameras, tubes, and stuff she couldn't even identify.

"You must be Abigail and Benjamin," said a little bald guy in a white button-down shirt. As he trundled up to them, Abby could see that he was actually shorter than Ben. "Now the question is, which one of you is Abigail, and which is Benjamin?"

He looked from Abby's face to Ben's, the light reflecting off his glasses.

"That's a joke, folks. A little humor to lighten up the moment. No harm done. I'm Monty. I run this lab. Come on in and meet everyone."

Lab?

Abby shot a glance at Ben. He was wearing an expression that said, "Is he for real?"

Monty the oddball was leading them to the center of the room, where two other kids were waiting with three other counselors, or teachers, or zookeepers, or whatever they were.

"The troops have arrived," Monty told his adult pals.

He introduced Abby and Ben to the others. Abby was happy to see that one of the other two kids in her group was Tabor, the kid from Hungary who could make a piece of paper fall off the edge of a table. *Of course he's in Telekinesis,* she thought. *He can't really move stuff with his mind—he moves stuff by bending his thumb—but close enough.*

The other kid was Reggie, a scrawny kid from Oklahoma who said he could make apple juice flow uphill.

"Really? That's so cool!" Ben said when he heard.

"It's actually not that cool," Reggie replied with a shrug. "It only goes up a tiny bit, and only if the angle isn't very big. Like if you tip up a cafeteria tray by putting a gummy bear under one end. Much steeper than that, and I can't get it to do anything."

At that moment, the door opened and a familiar blond head popped in. It was Phil Shutter, clutching, as always, a clipboard. He opened his mouth, and Kermit the Frog's voice came out.

"Okeydoke, folks! Sorry if I'm tardy; I've got a lot of rooms to visit," he began, approaching the group in the middle of the room.

"I just wanted to drop in and, you know, help you kick off the day's activities. And I hope you don't mind if I get just a tad bit serious for a moment." He took off his glasses, breathed on each lens to fog it up, and then wiped them with a white handkerchief.

"As you know, very few campers were selected to join us at this facility. Yes, it's an honor for you to be chosen, and you should be proud; but the greater honor is ours. Because the shepherds in this room—you might call them counselors, but we call them shepherds—have devoted their lives to exploring the boundaries of magic and science. I don't believe there's anyone else in the country who's better qualified to help you find out more about your abilities. What makes them tick, how to make them grow, how to help them become more powerful. And that's something we'd all like, right?"

A couple of the kids made polite "uh-huh" noises.

"In the next few days, we're going to lavish love and attention on you, in a way that I'll bet nobody's ever done before. We want you to feel as special as I'm certain you are. And in return, all I ask is that you give our shepherds your complete cooperation. We're all in this together, gang. Any questions?"

Yeah, a million, Abby thought. *I just don't know where to begin.*

"All-righty, then," Phil concluded. "Have a great morning." He turned on his heel and rushed out.

"All right, let's dig in," announced Monty, taking charge. "Benjamin, you'll be with Dr. Lansinger. She'll be your shepherd. Shake hands and say hello." Ben walked over to the lady with her hair in a bun and shook hands.

"Tabor, meet Dr. Davis—Dr. Davis, this is Tabor. Reggie, your shepherd is Dr. Wright here. And Abigail, you lucky girl, you're going to be stuck with me. Put 'er there."

He stuck out his bony hand. Abby shook it weakly.

"I understand you've got a certain affinity for *eggs*, am I right?"

Monty grinned his tight little grin and walked Abby over to a table at the side of the room. Her jaw dropped.

"What's all this?" she said. Of course, she could see perfectly well what it was: a little farmer's market of eggs. But not just white, regular, chicken eggs. Little blue robin's eggs. Big brown eggs. Smaller tan eggs. Tiny speckled ones. Even two huge eggs—ostrich, maybe.

"Well, our first job is to find the limits of your power," Monty began. "To find out just how far your skills can be expanded. I shall be by your side—the lucky shepherd who gets to see your special abilities blossom and grow!"

It was all Abby could do to understand what was happening; there was no time to figure out how she felt about it.

Monty sat down on one of the stools and opened a tiny

laptop, no larger than a paperback book. "We have two sets of everything here: your raw eggs, in the left-hand collection, and your hard-boiled, on the right. What do you say we begin with something that we know works well—the chicken's egg, hard-boiled?"

He reached over, plucked one out of its box, and set it on the table in front of her. And all of a sudden, he grew weirdly shy. "I, ah—I have to admit, Abigail, that I have not actually witnessed this power of yours myself. So it would be a great honor if you could, you know, ah . . . demonstrate."

"I actually prefer Abby," she said.

"I'm sorry?"

"Nobody calls me Abigail unless it's my mom and she's mad."

"Oh-ho! Yes, yes of course. Abby it is, and Abby it shall be. Forgive me. Abby. Yes. All right, then. Shall we begin?" And he gestured toward the hard-boiled egg on the table.

Abby sighed, reached up to her earlobes, and tugged them just enough to make the egg spin a few times.

"That's it," she said. "That's all it is."

"Correction," said Monty, tapping away on his computer. "That's all it is *so far*. Now we try . . . *this!*"

He snatched the egg away with his hand, then grabbed

a new one from the left-side pile. "And now: the un-cooked chicken's egg. Again, if you please."

"It won't work," Abby said. "I've tried it."

"Please—would you?" Monty gestured toward the egg.

Abby looked at the new egg and tugged her ears again. The egg did nothing.

"Fascinating," Monty said, typing. "It appears that cooking the egg affects its density and mass in such a way as to facilitate your influence. Yes. Yes."

He looked up. "All right then, moving on." He put the raw egg back in its box and put a tiny speckled one on the table. "Quail's egg." He tapped away on his keyboard.

Abby glanced around. She could see Ben sitting across the room, showing his key-flipping trick to his "shepherd," over and over again. By the window, Tabor was occupied the same way. His shepherd, a man with a wide face and bumpy skin, would balance a piece of paper or a card on the edge of the table, and Tabor would try to make it fall to the floor. And Reggie from Oklahoma was busily trying to make apple juice run uphill.

Monty cleared his throat. "Quail's egg. Shall we begin?"

Abby nodded and tried to make it spin. She couldn't.

She couldn't make the robin's egg spin, either. Or the finch egg. Or the sparrow egg. And definitely not the ostrich egg.

And that's how the morning went. Monty was always polite, always respectful, but Abby first grew bored and then impatient. Monty and the other shepherds seemed to be a lot more interested in the kids' dumb little powers than the kids were themselves.

At lunch, the kids spoke quietly as they chomped.

"I swear," Eliza was saying. "I'm like, 'Dudes! I can't levitate any higher than a quarter of an inch, okay?' And they're like, 'Oh, that's okay! Let's try tying you down with string! Let's try making you hold some heavy books! Let's try it if you start by standing on your head!' They think I'm, like, a balloon in the Macy's Thanksgiving Day Parade."

"I know," Abby responded, stabbing a bite of salad. "I had to tug my ears so many times, I feel like they're going to fall off my head."

Ben was more than grouchy; his mind hadn't stopped racing all morning.

"What I want to know is, what is this place, really? I mean, come on. You guys have seen our rooms—they're not cabins. And those shepherds aren't camp counselors, either. They're little science teachers. And all this stuff about—'Flip more than one key at once, Ben!' "

He shook his head and stared down at his cheeseburger. "I don't know what this place is, but I can tell you

179

that it's not a summer camp. And I swear, I'm going to find out what's—"

"BEN!" shouted Abby, interrupting him. "You're about to drip ketchup on your shirt."

She reached out toward him with her napkin. In fact, there wasn't any ketchup; she had noticed that Ferd was approaching the table with an overflowing tray of food. She thought Ben would probably prefer not to be overheard.

Ben caught on quickly. "Thanks, Abby," he said, looking at her with a half smile.

"Aloha, all," said Ferd. "So how was the first day of school?"

The kids smiled, but nobody said anything. They just kept right on eating.

Ferd sat down. "All right, my people. You've worked hard all morning, but your camp overlords have proposed something a little more enjoyable for the afternoon."

"You mean, like, shoveling dirt?" Eliza shot back.

Abby had to admit that Eliza was extremely good at sarcasm.

"The upstanding directors of this establishment have arranged for a little quality time in the big field behind the cafeteria—flying remote-control helicopters," he said. "Dogfights aren't out of the question."

"Remote-control helicopters?" It was Ricky (of course). He was so happy, he was about to splurt right out of his skin. "Can I try? Can I try?"

Abby smiled despite herself. She didn't care so much about flying the helicopters. But watching Ricky do it would be entertainment enough.

"Honey! E-mail from Abby!"

Mrs. Carnelia was sitting with her laptop on the living room couch, catching up on work. Abby's dad was just coming upstairs from the basement, wiping his hands on a rag. "Really? Great! Will you read it to me while I make some coffee?"

"Okay," she responded. "It goes like this."

And she read him the whole thing:

Received: July 1
From: acarnelia11@gmail.com
To: eastportmama@optonline.net
Subject: Howdy

Hey you guys,

Hey from your favorite daughter at super camp!

They just had a super-fun welcome party for all of us kids. There's about 25 of us from all over the country. They're all super-talented and really nice. They had a big cookout, and we all had a lot of fun. There are three other kids here from the camp I was at, including that guy Ben, who I think you met the first day.

How's everything with you guys? Does Ryan still have his frog?

I'm super-tired, so I'm going to sleep now . . . I'll e-mail some more after my first day tomorrow!

Love,
Abs

"Short and sweet," Mr. Carnelia said, coming over to sit next to his wife. "This place is in Pennsylvania, right?"

"So I'm told."

"Do we know where? What city?"

Mrs. Carnelia frowned. "Well, Abby didn't mention it. It might be in the paperwork somewhere."

She walked over to the bureau by the front door, where

a FedEx envelope of Cadabra materials had arrived the day before. She pulled out its contents, plucked out the shiny booklet titled "Camp Cadabra Advanced-Placement Summer Program," and stuffed the rest back into the envelope.

"Well, if the address is on this brochure, I can't find it," she said, sitting down again.

"It's not a big deal, munchkin," said Mr. Carnelia. "I was just wondering what sort of place it is. I mean, what does a camp look like when there are only twenty-five kids?"

And that's all they said about it that night. But Mrs. Carnelia was not completely comfortable.

Before she went to bed, she shot an e-mail message back to Abby.

Sent: July 1
From: eastportmama@optonline.net
To: acarnelia11@gmail.com
Subject: Re: Howdy

Dear Abby,

How wonderful to hear from you! Your dad and I are both so proud of you. We know you're going to have a wonderful experience, and we can't wait to hear more about the place.

For example: What is your room like? Do you have any roommates?

Are you getting enough sleep? Enough food? What does the place look like? Is it in a city, a suburb, or the countryside? What are your activities? Remember to use sunscreen if you're outside all day!

Ryan just started Adventure Camp at the Y . . . it's just mornings, from 8 a.m. until 1 p.m., but he's loving it.

Ryan no longer has the toad. I made him return it to the wilderness. The poor thing was not eating any of the bugs we caught for him (the toad, not Ryan).

Write back, and give us more details!

Love,
Mom

P.S. Where in Pennsylvania is the super camp?

CHAPTER

18

Spygirl

THE SECOND DAY OF SUPER CAMP began just like the first: Abby spent her morning in the Telekinesis lab with Monty and the other kids with pointless powers.

This time, Monty tried to see if she could make an egg spin by tugging on only one ear instead of two. By tugging with her eyes closed. By looking at the egg in a mirror. By crossing her arms and tugging opposite ears.

The answer, every time, was no. But to Abby's growing annoyance, Monty never gave up.

Accept it, Monty, she thought. *There's nothing more to this. What you see is what you get. And the sooner you understand that, the sooner you'll quit wasting your time. And mine.*

After about a half an hour, she asked if she could go to

the bathroom. "Of course," Monty replied. "But you'll need a security card to get in. I'll walk you over there."

Abby thanked him, and the two of them walked down the long hallway to the restrooms. Monty swiped his card across the black box by the women's room door, and the lock popped open.

As Abby pushed her way in, Monty leaned against the wall. "I'll wait here for you," he said.

"You don't have to," Abby responded. "I know the way back."

A few minutes later, Abby began her walk back to the Telekinesis room. But she wasn't in any particular rush.

She decided to treat herself to a little sightseeing. There was a tall, thin window in each door of the hallway. It might be interesting, she thought, to see what the other campers were up to.

There were three kids in the Metamorphosis lab. From her position in the hallway, Abby couldn't tell exactly what was going on. But she did see a huge, football-player kid at the nearest table.

Or, rather, on the nearest table. He was on his hands and knees, as though he were playing horsey. She caught a glimpse of bright yellow coming from his fist; it was a dandelion. But as he bobbed his head up and down, Abby gasped to see that the yellow dandelion was slowly turning into a different kind of dandelion—the puffy, delicate kind made of those little gray whiskery things that fly away when you blow on them.

"Neat trick," she said quietly to herself.

Across the hall was the Teleportation room. She peeked in. Nobody was in there at all.

She looked into Invisibility, too. Nobody there, either. *At least not that I can see,* Abby thought with a wry smile.

In the Body Morph room, she spotted Doreen, the girl who could raise her body temperature by two degrees. Doreen's "shepherd" was right in the middle of sticking a digital thermometer into Doreen's ear.

What a bummer, Abby thought, *to have a power that nobody even knows you have unless they stick a thermometer into you.*

But right across from Doreen, Abby could see a funny-looking kid she hadn't seen before. He was playing a harmonica, looking miserable, and resting his elbows on a table that was absolutely covered with crumpled-up, used Kleenexes. A shepherd wearing a light green shirt kept pulling new tissues out of a box and handing them to the kid, who would blow his nose into them and then throw them on the table. Over and over again.

I don't even want to know, thought Abby. She moved on.

She spotted Ricky in Weather Phenomena—good old Ricky. There he was, standing in front of two shepherds, each one holding up a mirror about six feet away. She couldn't hear anything through the door, but she knew

187

that if she could, she'd hear Ricky doing his counting by twos in Spanish. She could even guess what they were testing at the moment—whether he could fog up two mirrors at once. Ricky was clearly doing his best. Abby smiled in sympathy.

There was one other camper in the room with him: a very tall, very pretty teenage girl whose arms were covered in mud almost up to her shoulders. Abby couldn't really figure out what was going on, but it had something to do with stuffed animals.

She peeked into the ESP window. *This should be good,* she thought. She already knew that ESP stood for Extra-Sensory Perception—mind reading.

There were three campers in this room. Two of them, with their shepherds, were just sitting and watching the third one—a very young kid, maybe even a fourth-grader, standing up on a stool and saying something out loud.

The shepherd was looking embarrassed and red in the face. Abby hoped that the camper had just read the shepherd's mind and discovered something very, very private.

On the third night, after dinner, Abby decided not to go to the movie that the camp offered each night. She was tired, especially after the game of laser tag that all the campers had played that afternoon.

So she hung out in her room and checked her e-mail. Something from home!

Received: July 3
From: eastportmama@optonline.net
To: acarnelia11@gmail.com
Subject: Re: Howdy

Dear Abby,

How wonderful to hear from you! Your dad and I are both so proud of you. We know you're going to have a wonderful experience.

Ryan just started Adventure Camp at the Y . . . it's just mornings, from 8 a.m. until 1 p.m., but he's loving it.

Ryan no longer has the toad. I made him return it to the wilderness. The poor thing was not eating any of the bugs we caught for him (the toad, not Ryan).

Love,
Mom

Abby read the note a second time, her lips pursed into a frown. Her mom's e-mails were usually a lot chattier. And no "P.S.?" Her mom *always* ended her e-mails with a "P.S." or two (or three).

She must have been especially busy that day, Abby thought. So she clicked the Reply button and wrote back:

Sent: July 3
From: acarnelia11@gmail.com
To: eastportmama@optonline.net
Subject: Update from your daughter

Dear Mom and Dad and Ryan,

Hi guys—thanks for the e-mail! I miss youuuuuuuuuuuu!

Everything's OK here, but it's a very strange place. We spend every morning in these sort of science labs, with people named Dr. This and Dr. That poking us and asking questions and running a million experiments.

My friend Ben says it's nothing like the magic camps he's ever been to. They don't actually teach you any new magic. There are no performances or anything. You would think they might even have a professional magician come by every now and then! But they don't even do that.

Every morning we're in those science classrooms, and then in the afternoon, we do something fun. It's usually something high-tech, like flying remote-control helicopters or playing laser tag or shooting off model rockets.

The food's really good.

Whassup with you guys? When does Dad have to fly off somewhere again?

Love,
Abs

On the fourth day of super camp, Abby Carnelia finally began to guess what kind of trouble she was in.

That morning, two things shattered any illusions she still had that she was at any kind of normal summer camp.

The first thing happened just after five in the morning,

when she was still deep asleep. She was in the middle of a perfectly pleasant dream, something about winning a clarinet contest with a clarinet that could play itself, when the place went nuts. It started with a deafening alarm: "NAAAAK! NAAAAK! NAAAAK!" Abby jumped out of bed and poked her head into the hallway, where bright lights were flashing. She could see other kids peeking out, too, covering their ears, looking around, freaked out and confused.

Ferd waddled into view, wearing a tiger-striped bathrobe that wasn't quite tied securely enough. Some black-shirted helpers raced down the hallway.

"IS IT A FIRE DRILL?" Abby yelled to Ferd.

He nodded. "OR A SYSTEM TEST. NOTHING TO WORRY ABOUT."

A minute later, the sounds and lights turned off. The place was quiet once more, although Abby could hear some chatter from sleepy campers down the hallway.

Ferd held up his hands and shouted as he walked through the building. "Apologies, my people," he said. "They do these system tests now and again. Forgive the ungodly hour of the night. Now, back to bed with you!"

Abby wished that Ben were there so she could at least exchange *do-you-believe-this-guy?* looks with him. But the door to his room remained closed.

The second disturbing event came later, during the morning session. One by one, each kid was pulled out of class and taken into a little medical office for a checkup by the camp doctor. It was the full deal: they took Abby's temperature, looked in her ears and her nose, tapped her knee with a reflex hammer, wrapped one of those blood-pressure sleeves around her arm, weighed her and measured her.

And then they got ready to take a blood sample.

I don't know if you've ever had that done to you, but you probably wouldn't enjoy it. It's like getting a shot. Except instead of squirting some medicine into you, the needle pulls some blood out of you. If you're brave enough to watch, you actually see your blood going into the clear part of the syringe.

Abby *hated* shots, just hated them. She always had. Once, when she was five, her mom buckled Abby into the car to take her for a checkup—and then made the mistake of mentioning that she would have to get a shot. Abby jumped out of the car, ran out of the garage, scrambled inside the house, and hid herself in the closet in the attic. She didn't come out all day, no matter how much her parents called her name, no matter how hungry she got. They didn't find her until nearly dinnertime, when Abby finally came out. And that was only because she had to go to the bathroom so badly she was about to explode.

193

Abby could not understand why the camp doctor needed some of her blood, anyway. Sure, she got weighed and measured once in a while at school, but this was ridiculous.

"It's just to keep you healthy," the doctor kept saying. "Every camper gets a free checkup. It's all part of the program."

"But why do I need a shot?" Abby insisted.

"Listen, not everything at summer camp is supposed to feel good," the doctor said as he worked. "What about those early-morning Polar Bear dives into the freezing-cold lake? What about running the half-marathon around the mountain? What about when you have to carry your canoe a mile across land to get to the next place in the river? Sometimes, you just gotta do what's good for you."

Abby looked at the doctor with a scrunched-up face. "We didn't do any of that at summer camp!"

"Well," the doctor replied, coming toward her with the needle, "that's how it was in my day. You kids today don't know how easy you have it."

Abby skipped the movie that night, too. She was starting to miss home and wanted to see if her mom had written back.

Yes!

Received: July 4
From: eastportmama@optonline.net
To: acarnelia11@gmail.com
Subject: Re: Update from your daughter

Dear Abby,

Thank you so much for the e-mail! Those afternoon activities sound like a lot of fun. I can tell you, we didn't have remote-control helicopters when I was in summer camp a hundred years ago!

What do you do in the mornings? Is that when they teach the magic classes?

Are you having a chance to perform at all? Do they bring in magicians to do shows, like they did in New Hampshire?

Dad's at home for another few days, then he has to fly off. He took Ryan to a Yankees game today in New York, which is a big deal for both of them. Personally, I'd rather stay home and watch the grass grow.

Love,
Mom

P.S.—Hope you're getting plenty of sleep and meeting some great people!

P.P.S.—Old Mrs. Teplitz across the street had puppies! (I mean her dog did.)

Abby smiled and leaned back in the chair.

But after a moment, a little voice in her head suggested that she read the message again. This time, she wasn't smiling. Something was really weird about her mom's note.

"What do you do in the mornings?" "Do they bring in magicians?"

Didn't you read my last e-mail? Abby thought. *I already told you that stuff!*

Abby was growing annoyed. Her mother must have stopped reading Abby's e-mail after about one sentence. Abby was a slow typist, so her mom should appreciate every single sentence—and not get distracted after ten seconds of reading!

At that moment, there was a knock on Abby's door.

"Who is it?"

"It's . . . um, it's Monty." But it was Ben's voice. Abby grinned as she stood up.

"What do you want, Monty?" she asked, walking toward the door.

"I want to see if you can spin an egg by tugging on my ears."

She laughed and opened the door. "Why, Benjamin. What a surprise," she said.

"Hello, Abby Cadabra," he said as he came in.

"I thought you went to the movie."

"Nah," Ben replied. "It's *Titanic II: The Voyage Home*. I've seen it, like, six times."

"I know. Me, too. I practically understand the plot by now."

Ben flopped down into a big leather swiveling chair by the window. He had brought along a foam-rubber football. And now, as he swiveled the easy chair back and forth, he was absentmindedly tossing the football straight up into the air and catching it.

"So how are you enjoying super camp?" he asked.

Abby stopped and looked at him. Then she looked around. Without a sound, she walked over to the bed and pressed the button on the wall that made the TV screen rise up out of the dresser.

"What are you doing?" Ben asked, bewildered.

"Let's watch some TV! Can you grab the remote by your foot?" She turned on the TV and flicked through the channels until she found a concert video.

It was the Badd Boyz, singing their hit song, "U R 2 Good 4 Me":

Ooh baby, can't U C
That U R 2 good 4 me,
Ooo, honey I want yo touch,
But girl, U R way 2 much . . .

Abby turned it up loud.

"Auuuggh!" Ben shouted, trying to make his voice heard over the music. "Okay, first, I can't stand that song. And second, if I wanted to watch TV, I would have stayed in my own room!"

She put a finger to her lips, in a *Shhhh!* motion. Then she dragged the desk chair across the rug until it was right next to Ben's easy chair and sat down.

"I just want to make sure they can't hear us," she said.

"Who?"

"You know, in case they've got little microphones hidden around, and they're listening to us."

Ben studied her with curiosity. "Do you really think?"

"I'm sorry. I don't trust these people. They took blood

from us today! This isn't a super camp—it's a super lab. And we're their guinea pigs." She looked away. "I know. You think I'm completely paranoid."

"Actually, I don't," he said. "I thought I was the only one."

Abby looked at him sharply.

"Why? Did you find out something?"

"Well, let me just ask you this: What's the deal with all the security?"

Abby shrugged. "They said it's to keep us safe from outsiders."

"Nope," Ben replied. "It's to keep us in."

Okay, that's a little creepy, thought Abby.

"Why do you think that?" she asked.

"You'll see," he said, glancing around. He brushed his floppy hair off his forehead, the way he always did. But this time, she could see that his eyes were especially intense.

"You know how I never show up at breakfast?" he said. "They think I'm a slacker, or maybe just a little unpredictable. But it's great because they leave me alone so I can do a little exploring."

"What kind of exploring?"

"Well, like this morning, I woke up super-early, for some reason, so I decided to see how hard it would be to get outside. Not inward, into the courtyard, but the other way. Out of this place. So I went past the reception desk where Candi sits. I don't have one of those security cards, but I didn't need one; someone had left the first set of doors open. So I just walked right through them, down the hall toward the doors to the main building, when all of a sudden—"

"What?" Abby asked, spellbound.

"It was like: 'BAAAAMP! BAAAAMP!' These alarms went off!"

Abby lit up. "Oh, yeah! We heard that! Like in the middle of the night! That was you?"

"Yeah," Ben said. "That was me. And they have these metal gates that come down from the ceiling, just like in the movies. Both ends of the hallway. It scared the heck out of me."

"So what happened?"

"Well, I was trapped in there! I couldn't get out either end of the hallway. I was in there for, like, five minutes before three of those helper guys could open the gates again and let me back in."

"Well, what made the alarm go off? Did someone push a button or something?"

"I don't think so," Ben replied. "It went off right when I started walking down the hall. Didn't Phil say something about motion detectors or pressure sensors in the floor? Just stepping into that hallway makes the alarms go off."

Abby frowned. "But didn't we come in that way on the first day? There wasn't any alarm then."

"I know," Ben said. "They probably turn themselves off during the day. They must be on a timer."

"So what did you say when they caught you?"

Ben grinned. "I pretended to wake up. Like I'd been sleepwalking."

"Are you kidding me?" Abby had always known that Ben was a daredevil, but she couldn't believe his guts this time. "Did they believe it?"

He nodded. "I think so. Since the day we got here, I've sort of been letting them think that I'm a little loopy."

"Oh, like you're really not?"

She grinned at him. But inside, her feelings were anything but cheerful.

CHAPTER
19
Darkening

IF YOU REALLY WANT to be totally accurate about it, the day that really changed the direction of Abby's life wasn't the day she discovered her power.

It was the day Ben sang to her in the Telekinesis lab.

Ben had now been an impostor at the super camp for six days. His key-flipping trick was so good, it had everyone convinced that it was a real supernatural power (although a pretty pointless one). Ben kept telling Abby that he was sure he was going to be discovered at any moment—but so far, nobody had suspected.

The sixth day in the lab was no more interesting to Abby than the other days had been. Monty had brought in some scientific machines to see if he could figure out what kind of force she was actually applying to that egg. "To see the unseen!" he said, holding one finger up in the air. "This is our challenge today!"

It took him most of an hour to figure out how to set up the thermography camera, which was supposed to be able to make what Monty called "heat movies." It was like a huge, ridiculously clumsy camcorder, except that it didn't measure light; it measured heat.

On the screen, Abby could see cool areas in black or blue, medium areas in green, and then warmer areas—like her face and hands—in shades of orange and yellow. She moved around, dancing in front of the lens, watching her weird, rainbowy shape on the screen. When she exhaled hard, she saw a spray of hot orange shoot out of her mouth, as though she were a girl dragon.

When Monty aimed the camera at the egg on the counter, though, it was just green—and stayed that way, even while it was spinning.

Monty looked unhappy. After a few more tries, he sighed deeply, and then he began taking the machine apart again.

"All right, you kids stay right here," he said glumly. "I'm going to go get the magnetic resonance camera. Dr. Lansinger?"

Dr. Lansinger, Ben's shepherd, had been spending the

week trying to explore the bounds of Ben's key trick. But she hadn't made any progress with him, either. He couldn't seem to make anything flip but the key. He couldn't make the key flip anywhere but on his hand. And he couldn't make it do anything but flip once.

Because the magnetic resonance camera was heavy, Monty asked her to help him wheel it into the Telekinesis lab. While both shepherds were out of the room, Ben ambled over to Abby's table.

"Yo, Abby Cadabra," he said, hoisting himself up to sit on the table's edge.

"Hey," said Abby. She was feeling a little bored—and a little down.

"You were making some awfully cool rainbow movies there. I saw you breathe out that orange and yellow air. That never happens to me, except sometimes after I eat Mexican food."

She smiled despite herself.

He glanced toward the door and then looked back at Abby. "Hey. Is something the matter?"

Abby didn't respond for a moment.

"Come on," he prodded. "You can tell me."

She sighed. "It's just—I don't know. This place is wearing me down. It's not what I had in mind when I signed up for summer camp."

"That's because it's not a summer camp," he said. "There's more to this. I'm sure of it."

He picked up Monty's clipboard and looked down at it.

"Man, oh man," he said. "Check this out." He pulled a sheet of paper out from under the spring clip. "Look at this—the dude's taking notes on us, like a scientific study. You were right when you said we're guinea pigs."

"Shhhh!" Abby said, with a nervous glance at the other two shepherds in the room. "They'll hear you."

"Oh, don't worry about that," Ben replied. "I can just turn up the music!"

And that's when he started to sing. Pretty badly, actually.

"Ooh baby, can't U C, that U R 2 good 4 me! Ooh, honey, I want your touch—but girl, U R way 2 much!"

Abby screamed. It was more of a yelp, actually. Still, it was so loud, everybody in the room stopped what they were doing and stared.

They saw her standing next to Ben, her hands stuffed into her mouth as though to silence her own reaction.

"What's the matter?" Ben said. "What happened?"

Dr. Wright, one of the other shepherds in the room, hurried over. "What's the trouble, Abby?"

She thought fast. "Nothing—nothing," she said. "I—I bit my tongue. I always do that when I'm talking too fast. I'm really sorry."

"Should we have the nurse take a look?" Dr. Wright said, genuinely concerned.

Abby shook her head. "No, no, it's just fine. It's already fine. Thank you so much."

"All right. Well, you let us know if you want someone to look at it." Dr. Wright smiled and returned to his own table.

Ben waited until he was out of earshot. "What was *that* about?" he whispered urgently.

"Look."

She pointed at the page in his hand, the one covered with Monty's notes.

"What? It's just his notes," Ben said.

"But it was white before. The paper was white. *Really* white. I saw it. I saw it change! It changed right in your hand."

Ben held the page up. It wasn't white, exactly. It was just a hair darker, a very faint gray, as though it had moved from sunshine into shadow.

"It looks the same to me."

"Here, then," she said. She was suddenly filled with energy and a sense of purpose. She grabbed the clipboard from Ben's hands and pulled off another sheet of paper.

"Here. Hold this and do it again," she told Ben.

"Do what?"

"What you did before! Sing that song!"

He stared at her. "Are you kidding me? I was just goofing around! I was just—"

"*Sing it!*"

Ben could see that he wasn't going to win this one. So he started singing that annoying Badd Boyz song again, the one he couldn't stand, the one that had been running through his head since the night before.

He didn't have much energy this time, and he wasn't very loud, and his attention was on the sheet of paper. But he sang.

"Ooh baby, can't U C . . . that U R 2 good 4 me! Ooh, honey, I want your touch—"

He stopped singing—and breathing. Because he saw it, too. The piece of paper in his hand had just gotten a shade darker. Right in front of him. Unmistakably. In a blink.

His jaw dropped as he met Abby's gaze. She was nodding, her face glowing with happiness.

"Ben! *You have a power!*"

"Wait, what?"

She grabbed his sleeve. "Don't you get it? You *do* have a power after all! You've just never known it. Because you've never found the trigger! It has something to do with that song, or something—I don't know. But it's real. You're not just a fake magician after all!"

Ben was still trying to process all of this.

"That's—a *power?*" he said. "Making a piece of paper turn light gray? But you can barely see it!" He was holding the light gray page against another piece of paper on the clipboard so that he could see them side by side.

"Yes, but don't you see? *All* our powers are stupid! They're *all* sort of ridiculous. But it doesn't matter. You're still changing the laws of nature. You're still doing something that nobody else in the world can do."

And that, she thought to herself, *makes you special. Absolutely, incredibly special.*

Ben shook his head, as though he was trying to shake himself awake. "But come on. What could that stupid pop song have to do with anything? Why would it be that one song? What if I'd never heard it? What if it had to be a pop song in another country? What if it were never written?"

Abby shrugged. "Then you'd never have discovered your power." She yanked another pair of pages from the clipboard. "Here. Do it again! One more time—please?"

Ben did as he was told, this time with a growing smile. Once again, he sang—and once again, the pages darkened in his hand.

The door opened, and they could see the unmistakable shape of Monty's rear end backing through it. He was tugging the front end of a cart; Dr. Lansinger was pushing from the other side. Another piece of scientific equipment sat on top.

As quickly as she could, Abby grabbed the pages, squared them up, and put them back onto the clipboard. Ben hopped off the table edge, his mind still in a daze. Abby grabbed his shoulder and leaned forward.

"Don't tell," she whispered. He looked back at her and nodded before walking back to his table.

Abby spent the rest of the morning tolerating Monty's experiments, but her mind was somewhere else. Not only had Ben never had any real powers before, but it had taken him a long time to believe that anyone *else* had them.

And yet, when all the circumstances were just right, he'd found his magic. He'd found the power he'd always had, locked away inside, waiting for the one moment when all the conditions for his trigger were lined up exactly.

That's what happened to Eliza. And Ricky. And Tabor. And Doreen.

And me.

Until the day they discovered their powers, how were they any different from normal kids?

We weren't. All it took was a freak of chance, when we stumbled upon our powers.

Ben's discovery was turning Abby's brain inside out. The question she couldn't shake was: *Are we the only ones with powers?*

Or is there something waiting to be discovered inside every kid on earth?

CHAPTER
20
Truck

ABBY HADN'T EVEN RECOVERED from the first shock of the day when she got another one. And it started with round-headed Ricky.

"Does anybody know what we're doing after lunch?" he asked between taco bites. The afternoons were always his favorite. The afternoons were *everyone's* favorite. Not only was there always something fun to do, but there was no testing or examining at all.

"No clue," said Ben.

"Maybe we can go to the farm," Ricky responded. "I really wanna go see it."

Eliza made a face. "What farm? There's no farm."

"There is, too," said Ricky. "I saw one of the trucks go by."

"What trucks?" asked Abby. Her room had a view of the inner courtyard, but Ricky's window faced the side of the central building. A driveway ran past it.

"One of their trucks. It said 'Good Farma for Those We Love.'" He wiped some salsa off of his tray with a napkin.

"You mean 'good farmers?'" asked Abby.

"Probably it just said, 'good farms,'" said Ben.

"I'll bet it was 'good farming,'" offered Eliza.

"No!" said Ricky, getting cranky. "It said 'Good Farma.' I'm very observant. I notice these things. I'm a good speller." He sipped from the straw in his chocolate milk. "And the farmers are not," he said after a moment.

Abby didn't get it. "Are not what?"

"Are not good spellers," said Ricky. "They had two spelling mistakes on the same truck."

"What were they?" Ben wanted to know.

"Well, 'Good Farma,' for one thing. They spelled Farma with a P-H, like in phantom."

"That's not a spelling mistake, you dingbat," said Eliza. She adjusted a fold of her huge tie-dyed T-Shirt. "That's just how you spell pharma. As in, 'pharmaceutical.' As in, 'medicines and drugs.' My dad used to be a lawyer for a pharma company. That's how I know." She turned and gave Ricky a mock pat on the shoulder. "Hate to break it to you, Ricky, boy, but there's no farm around here. You saw a drug-company truck."

Abby smiled. *Good old Ricky.* "What was the other spelling mistake, Ricky?" she asked.

Ricky was feeling a little hurt by Eliza's comment. He wasn't especially enthusiastic about sharing the second misspelling he'd seen, just in case he was wrong about that one, too.

"Well, maybe it wasn't," was all he said. He picked up another carrot stick.

"C'mon, you can tell us," said Abby. "We're not gonna laugh at you. *Are* we, Eliza?"

Eliza rolled her eyes at Abby, but said nothing.

"Tell us, Ricky," Ben prodded.

Ricky looked out the window, then back at the other kids. "Oh, all right. The big letters on the truck said 'Calabra' instead of 'Cadabra.'" He glared at Eliza. "Did your *dad* work for *that* company, too?"

"No," she replied. "But that's not a typo, either. There *is* a company called Calabra. Don't you guys's parents give you Armadrol when you get sick?"

"Mine do," said Ricky.

"Yep. Calabra makes it. They have ads on TV all the time." Eliza shrugged. "So it's not much of a coincidence that a Calabra truck has an ad on it that talks about 'Good Pharma.'"

Ben made eye contact with Abby. "But it's a little weird

212

that a truck that says *Calabra* is driving around a camp called *Cadabra*, isn't it? I mean, that's quite a coincidence."

Eliza shrugged and swallowed a bite of ravioli. "Depends on whether you're freaked out by coincidences all the time."

"Are you saying there's no farm, for sure?" Ricky looked genuinely disappointed.

"There's no farm," said Abby gently.

But it sure would be nice if there were, she thought.

"Are you thinking what I'm thinking?" Abby asked Ben as they walked out of the cafeteria.

"I certainly hope not," he said with a grin. "I don't want any part of what's going on in your twisted mind."

"Come on, Ben," she pleaded. "What Ricky said. What's a drug truck doing driving around this camp?"

"I don't know—bringing supplies to the infirmary? They're big into taking blood samples and having doctors fussing over us. If you hadn't noticed."

She shook her head. "Ben, there's something creepy going on here. I know it. And I know how to find out what it is."

They were passing through the central lobby that connected their rooms. She and Ben both gave a little wave to

213

Candi, who was sitting at her desk as usual, typing away on her computer. They waited by the hallway, as they did every day, until Ferd could come and take them outside to the afternoon activity.

Ben lowered his voice until he was almost whispering. "Okay, what?"

"We need to look on Candi's computer."

Ben laughed. "Since when did you turn into Abby the Spy? Come on. There's no way."

"Why not?"

Ferd chose that moment to burst through the double doors. Eliza and Ricky were already with him.

"Okay, kidlets. Let's motivate. We've got a major Ultimate Frisbee war brewing out on the back lawn."

Abby and Ben followed the group outside. But as they walked out onto the grass, they hung back far enough that they could continue their conversation in private.

"Why can't we see what's on Candi's PC?" Abby asked, more urgently now. It seemed like such a natural way to find out what made Camp Cadabra tick.

"Well, for one thing, there's probably a password about six feet long," he said. "This isn't like *Mission: Impossible*, where you can just guess what the password is."

"Can't we try, though? Please? Just try?"

"Try how? You'd have to get her away from there."

"So we'll try after she leaves at night! Come on, Ben, you're good at all that techie stuff."

"But I'm not a hacker." Ben, for the first time since Abby had known him, was dragging his feet. "Look, Abby. I'm already not supposed to be here. It just doesn't seem right. I don't want to get caught; I'd be in so much trouble."

Abby hung her head in discouragement. Her deep brown hair fell over her face.

"Look, Abby. We're only going to be here for a few more days, and then the whole thing will be behind us."

She gave him a tight little smile. "Okay," she said.

But it wasn't.

&

The movie that night was *Dr. Doolittle IV: Llama's Revenge*. Abby joined the other kids, but only reluctantly; her mind was elsewhere. She sat in the back row, and after ten minutes, she decided that the popcorn was actually more interesting than the movie.

Fortunately, things got more interesting very fast.

"Abby."

It was Ben, standing behind her chair and whispering in her ear. He was out of breath.

"What?"

"I gotta talk to you. Come outside for a sec."

She stepped up on the seat's armrest and climbed over the back of the chair. The two of them walked out the back of the movie theater—actually a small auditorium that was normally used for speeches—and into the vestibule.

"Come 'ere," Ben said. "Sit here for a second." He gestured to a half-wall by the big picture windows.

She sat. "What? What is it?"

"Okay. Well, remember how you said I should snoop around on Candi's computer?"

She nodded.

"Well, I couldn't do that. I watched her this afternoon when she was on the phone; the screen saver comes on after five minutes, and you need a password to get back in. But it gave me an idea."

Abby's eyes were wide. She leaned forward. "What? Tell me!"

Ben waggled his eyebrows, enjoying every minute of this.

"Okay. So we see Candi every day, when we go in and out of our rooms, right? But hardly anyone ever talks to her. So I decided to chat her up a little. Turns out she's really nice. She's twenty-five, she grew up about ten miles from here, she has a boyfriend, she's been working here for eight months."

Abby kept waiting for the punch line. "You dragged me out of the movie to tell me about Candi's love life?"

"No, no. I'm just telling you what happened. Okay, so

after a minute, she asks if I'm having a good time here, and I tell her, sure. Except I tell her that I'm a little insecure about my trick. I tell her, all the other kids have much cooler powers than me. And she's like, 'Oh, no, I doubt that very much!' And she asks to see it! She asks if she can see my power!"

He looked at Abby, waiting for her reaction. But she didn't have one. Not yet.

"Don't you get it? She asked to see my trick! This is perfect! So I said, 'Sure. I do it with a key, like a house key or a car key. Do you have one? And so she says, 'Yeah—here's the one for the desk drawers, but I need it right back!' "

Now Abby got it. She giggled with excitement. "No way! She gave you her desk key?"

"Yeah. And you know what? It's one of those copper ones with a jagged edge, just like my house key! So I did a palm switch!"

"A what?"

Ben hadn't meant to confuse her with magicians' mumbo jumbo. "A palm switch! I did my trick for her, and she thought it was really great—but then I gave her back the wrong one!"

"What do you mean?"

"I wound up with . . . Oh, hey wait! You've got something in your ear?"

He reached past the side of her head and pretended to pull something out of her ear. It was the oldest, dumbest trick in the book—but she gasped when she saw what was in his fingers.

"You got her desk key!"

"It may not be as good as hacking into her computer, but it may be fun to see where it leads anyway. You game?"

Abby was excited now, fired up by the thrill of the hunt.

"Of course I am! Let's go!"

They scurried out to the central atrium where Candi's desk sat empty in the dim light. They hunched down behind it, right next to its locked fake pinewood doors.

Ben handed her the key. "You're the mastermind; *you* do it."

Abby slipped the key into the lock and turned it. The desk door swung open easily. And inside was—a bunch of papers and folders.

Well, what did you expect? said the little voice in her head. *A stash of weapons?*

Abby grabbed a handful of pages, knelt on the ground, and started reading them out loud.

"Cadabra Movie Schedule. Vegetarian Cafeteria Menu. Shepherd Contact List. Emergency Evacuation Protocols. Employee Pension Plan Information . . ."

She looked up at Ben, confused. "What is all this?"

"I don't know. Just a bunch of general stuff for Candi or whoever works here, I guess."

Abby kept flipping through the pages, her excitement

quickly turning to boredom. "Vacation Policy. Annual Federal Holidays. Philadelphia Metropolitan Bus Schedule."

She sighed and stacked up the pages, ready to put them back in the desk. "Forget it," she said. "There's nothing juicy in here."

But Ben put his hand on her wrist. "Wait a sec. Go back. Right where you stopped. What was that?"

She flipped past all the same pages again until she found what he wanted. "This? Camper Research Schedule?" She pulled it out of the stack.

"Yeah. That's gotta be about us, right?"

Abby started reading it out loud.

"6/30. Evening welcome barbecue. 6–9 p.m., courtyard. No research. 7/1. Morning introductions, meet shepherds, begin exploration of talents."

She looked up. "It *is* about us. It's just our schedule."

"Yeah, but—" He was reading intently over her shoulder. "What's that? Look what it says down there!"

She scanned down the page. "7/8. Primary medical staff arrives. Begin Level 2 research: hypnotherapy, medication, MRI/CAT scans. 7/10. Minor exploratory surgery on selected subjects. Harvest tissue samples."

She read it again to herself, not quite understanding. But even if her brain wasn't grasping it all, her gut was telling her plenty. A cold, dark shadow passed through her.

"What is all this?" she asked, barely daring to breathe.

"I'm pretty sure it's what they have planned for us next, Abby."

He met her gaze. Abby saw uncertainty and fear on Ben's face for the very first time, and it made her even more afraid. She felt as though her stomach had just dropped right down out of her body.

When she was capable of taking another breath, she finally spoke. "What are they going to do to us, exactly?"

Ben took the page from her. He looked down at it, partly to read it again and partly because he didn't want her to see what he was feeling.

"Well, you know. Hypnotherapy? That's hypnosis. They're gonna hypnotize us. A CAT scan is where they stick you into this huge tube that can, like, take pictures of your brain and your guts and stuff. Medication means giving us pills or shots."

"But why do they have to do all that?"

"And you know what surgery is," he finished up.

Abby's eyes flashed with anger. Doctor stuff, blood, taking pills—all that stuff had always made her queasy even when it was supposed to make her *healthy*. But there was nothing wrong with her now—and the thought of being unconscious and even operated on for no reason at all was so upsetting, her hands started to shake.

She grabbed his forearm. "They're not gonna make *me* do that stuff!"

Ben nodded. "I'm sure any of the kids here would agree with you. The thing is, they weren't going to *tell* us any of this. They're just planning to *do* it. So we wouldn't have a choice!"

"Well, they're not gonna do that to me! I swear to God. I'll run away."

He sighed. "Well, actually, what I want to do first is have a little chat with our buddy Phil Shutter. I think he owes us some explanation. You want to come with me?"

She stood up and handed the folder back to him. "*Want* to? A whole army couldn't keep me away."

"Great. We'll hunt him down right after breakfast tomorrow."

When Abby got back to her room, she turned on the gleaming laptop on the desk. She fired up her e-mail program and wrote:

Sent: July 6
From: acarnelia11@gmail.com
To: eastportmama@optonline.net
Subject: URGENT!!!!!!

Dear Mom and Dad and Ryan,

I don't think you know what this place is. They are treating us like science projects! On Monday,

they're gonna do stuff like hypnotizing us,
giving us shots, and sticking us in scanning
tubes. And even surgery!! Did you have any
idea that this stuff was going to go on?

I want to come HOME!

Can you at least call here and make them let me
talk to you? I really, really don't want to be here
anymore. I'm going to talk to the guy who runs
it tomorrow. I'm going to tell him I'm homesick
and need to leave.

I'm really scared, you guys. I never expected
any of this.

Please, please write back.

Love you!
Abs

She read over it one more time and then clicked Send.
    She went to bed, but it was hours before she finally fell
into a shallow, fitful sleep.

CHAPTER
21
Phil

Eastport, Connecticut, was in the middle of a gigantic summer rainstorm the next morning—"the storm of the century," the guy on the news channel kept saying.

Then again, he had also said that about the last storm, and the one before that.

Mrs. Carnelia made breakfast for her husband and Ryan, and then sat down at her desk to check her e-mail. After a moment of reading, she stood up, frowning. "Jack?" she called. "Jack, come in here a sec. I think you should see this!"

Mr. Carnelia poked his head into the study. "What is it, hon?"

She pointed to the screen. "Take a look at this note from Abby."

Received: July 7
From: acarnelia11@gmail.com
To: eastportmama@optonline.net
Subject: Hello!

Dear Mom and Dad and Ryan,

this.

Please, please write back.

Love you!
Abs

He read it over, then ran his hand over his scalp. "Well, that's not like the Abbmeister," he said. "It's too short."

"It's not just that," his wife pointed out. "The truth is, I've been writing her back immediately, every time I get a note from her. Why would she send a note that doesn't say anything but 'please write back'? And what's this one word by itself there?"

Mr. Carnelia turned to go. "I wouldn't worry about it, hon. She must have gotten interrupted in the middle of writing, or she deleted something by accident. Just write her back and ask. I'm sure it's fine—don't worry about it." And he slipped out.

But Mrs. Carnelia did worry. She hit Reply and typed:

Sent: July 7
From: eastportmama@optonline.net
To: acarnelia11@gmail.com
Subject: Re: Hello!

Abby, honey!

Your last e-mail was so short and strange. Is
everything OK? What do you mean "please, please
write back?" I've replied to every e-mail you've
sent!

Please tell us if everything is OK. We miss you,
and can't wait to see you in one more week!

Love,
Mom

Phil Shutter's brain always seemed to be going in six di-
rections at once. At mealtimes, it was usually his habit to
flit from table to table, checking in with people, following up, getting ready for the day. So it wasn't hard for Ben
and Abby to find him at breakfast.

They waited, as politely as they could, until he was finished talking to one of the shepherds.

"Phil?"

He turned, beaming, opening his arms wide, as though he were going to hug them, and then changed his mind. "Ben and Abby! Good morning! Did you try the blueberry pancakes? They're fresh blueberries. This time yesterday, they were still on the bushes!"

Ben ignored the question. "Hey, do you have a minute after breakfast? We have something sort of serious we need to talk to you about."

Phil went into Fake Caring mode, the way grownups do when you're four years old and crying because you can't find your teddy bear.

"Oh, dear dear dear, I'm sorry to hear that! Not *too* serious, I hope? But by all means, by all means. My door is always open, you know that. You're my Number One priority! We can meet in my office. I'll have Ferd show you the way. How's that?"

He smiled and gave each of them a weird little double pat on the shoulder.

"Okay . . . thanks," said Ben unsteadily. "We'll see you in a little bit."

And that was that. He and Abby returned to their table and didn't say much until breakfast was over.

"So you've secured a meeting with the big boss, eh?"

Ferd said as he escorted them through the building a few minutes later. "I trust you're not applying for a job here?" He was trying to kid around, but Abby and Ben were in no mood for it.

When they got to Phil's office, the door was locked; Ferd knocked, and Phil opened it a moment later. "Come in, come in! Please. Sit. Here." Phil indicated a couple of chairs across from his polished, walnut desk.

Abby scanned the office. She had to admit, it was absolutely beautiful. It was filled with shiny dark wood furniture, tall glass display cases, and high-tech gadgetry. There was a photo of two cute preschoolers on Phil's desk, and four framed diplomas hanging on the wall. There were also some paintings here and there.

Phil sat down, too. "Okeydoke! Now what can I do for you kids? Everything all right with the food?"

Ben and Abby shifted uncomfortably. Who was going to speak first?

It was Abby. "We'd like to know exactly what's going on here," she said.

Phil didn't bat an eye. "What's going on here? Well, I think you know the answer to that, Abby."

He smiled broadly. She freaked quietly.

"What's going on here is a one-of-a-kind, advanced-placement program for extremely gifted young magicians. Our mission is to nurture your skills, to explore the boundaries of your powers, and to make you proud to be a Camp Cadabra graduate!"

"No it's not." Abby's voice was low, with an intensity that surprised even her.

"No *what's* not?" asked Phil, pretending to be confused.

"That's not what this is all about, and you know it. And now *we* know it."

Phil slipped into his singsongy, talking-to-kinder-garteners voice. "Abby, Abby, Abby! I want you to know that I am a very decent guy. I've been a dedicated scientist for twenty years. I'm interested only in the truth. That's what scientists do. That's what—"

"We want to see your business card." Abby interrupted him in a way that would have earned her a dirty look from her mom. But she couldn't listen to Kermit the Frog tricking her for one more minute.

"I beg your pardon?"

"We want to see your business card."

"I don't think that's really important right now, Abby," said Phil. "What's important right now is—"

"Show her the darned card!" said Ben, almost yelling. "Or we're going to tell the whole world about what's really going on at this place."

Talk about a magic trick. Before Abby's eyes, Phil's happy, goofy, singsongy façade completely disappeared. "Don't you threaten me, young man," he said, his voice like a knife. "You don't have the first clue who you're dealing with."

Even so, Phil reached into his pocket, pulled out his wallet, and threw a business card onto the desk. Abby picked it up to read it.

"Philip M. Shutter, PhD," she read out loud. "Director of Product Development . . ."

And here she looked up to meet Phil's gaze, with intensity you hardly ever see in an eleven-year-old. ". . . Calabra Pharmaceuticals."

Phil didn't say anything.

"This isn't a summer camp, is it, Phil?" said Ben, finally. "It's a drug company."

Phil tilted his head back and dragged his hands down his own face before replying.

"Well, of *course* it's a drug company," he replied. "When have you ever seen a summer camp with facilities like this? When have you been to a summer camp with cabins or dining halls or—or *prices* like Cadabra? When have you ever stayed in rooms equipped like the ones you're staying in? How do you think we pay for all that? Not from your parents' camp money, I'll tell you that!"

"Wait," said Abby. She still didn't quite get what Calabra had to do with Cadabra. "So your company makes drugs, but you've made some kind of deal with magic camps all over the country?"

"Don't be silly," Phil replied, glaring at her. "We don't have *deals* with those magic camps. We *built* those magic camps! We *own* those magic camps! And we created the Cadabra camp system for one reason only: to find *you*."

Phil seemed to be energized once more. Kermit began to sneak back into his voice. "We realized that there are a few—very, *very* few children who have these gifts. These abilities. We are the only pharma company with the insight to embrace you—to find you, to bring you together. We support you. We care for you. We encourage you. We entertain you. We try to help you blossom!"

He was breathing hard now. "Actually, I have a question for *you*, Abby Carnelia. I would like to know what gives you the right to come storming in here, into my office, when we've done *nothing* but try to make your lives magical, every step of the way?"

Abby said nothing for a moment; she was a little scared. But she pulled herself together.

"You haven't explained *why* you're doing all this," she said.

"Why? I told you why. Because we love you! We want to make your lives special!"

Ben was getting impatient. "Okay, so if you want to make our lives special, then why are you going to hypnotize us?"

"And give us medicines, and stick us in a cat tube?" added Abby.

Phil looked back and forth between them. "Who told you that?" he asked, narrowing his eyes.

"Never mind," Ben said. "We just know it, okay? And you haven't answered the question: why?"

Phil's face looked knotted up, as though he couldn't believe he was being interrogated by two middle-schoolers.

"Look. After all I've done for you kids, I'm not going to sit here and entertain these unhealthy questions. I'm a busy man, and I've got a busy day ahead of me. This conversation is over."

"Okay, that's fine," said Abby. "I'll just write on my blog about how you keep us locked in here, with one-way doors so we can't get out. And how you won't let us call home so our parents don't know what's really going on here. And how you're turning children—little children, who can't defend themselves—into guinea pigs for your science experiments! How you're going to cut us up! Yep, I think the whole Internet should know about all that stuff. Don't you, Ben?"

"I sure do," said Ben, grinning. "I think they'd find it fascinating."

Phil made a tiny gurgle; it sounded as though there was an entire fish stuck in his throat. Then he exploded— "like a volcano," as Abby described it later.

"You just don't get it, do you?" He leaned forward on

his desk, supporting himself on both hands, and drilling into them with his eyes.

"This company is dedicated to *saving lives* and *helping people*," he spluttered. "I've spent twenty years helping this company find the next miracle cure, the next medicine that will help people. At this very moment, your grandparents are probably taking our pills so their arthritis won't hurt as much. Your fathers are probably alive because of our heart medicine. When you were babies and you got sick, your parents gave you our drops to help you stop coughing so you could sleep. How *dare* you treat me like I'm the enemy?"

Abby and Ben were frozen, too startled to move.

"You think we're the bad guys? We're the *good* guys! You want to know who the bad guys are? Do you?"

Abby nodded—a tiny, terrified nod.

"The bad guys are the *other* drug companies, the ones who copy our formulas. We spend a fortune to find the next miracle drug. You can't imagine how hard it is—how long it takes, how much money it takes—to discover some plant, some rare fern in some South American jungle. Then we have to figure out what it's good for, figure out how much to put in each pill, make sure it's safe! So finally it's ready. It saves thousands of lives, makes thousands of lives better. But then . . ."

Phil started to look pained, as though he had had a splinter in his finger for a week.

"But the law says that it's ours for only ten years. Ten years! After that, any company can copy our formulas, copy our medicines, and sell theirs cheaper. They're allowed to skip past all our hard work, our science, our discoveries. And do you know what that does? It makes it very hard for us to keep doing what we do. We have to keep coming up with new drugs, new medicines, new South American ferns, to replace the ones that the other companies are now copying."

He paused to take a deep breath. He looked off to the side, as though talking to himself. "And right now, we've got nothing in the pipeline."

Ben glanced at Abby. "What do you mean, pipeline?"

"I mean we've got nothing lined up. We don't have the next blockbuster pill, the next lifesaving drug. If we don't find something big, and something soon, there'll be nothing left to keep this company alive."

Abby almost felt sorry for the guy.

"But what does all of this have to do with us?"

"It has everything to do with you, Abby," Phil said. Suddenly, he seemed more tired than angry. He sat back down at last.

"You kids are the last hope. That's why we created the

camps. To find you, to bring you here to our headquarters. You can help us. You can help save thousands of lives! You may wind up helping your parents and your grandparents—even your children and grandchildren!"

"But how? How is my spinning an egg going to, you know, make my grandchildren get well?"

Phil sighed deeply. There was no longer any reason to hide the truth.

"Okay, Abby, here it is. I'm going to level with you. Now, you know and I know that there is something special about you kids. Something remarkable. Something the world has never seen before. These powers might seem useless and pointless to you. But no matter how tiny these powers are, they're changing the laws of nature.

"We don't know how you're different from everyone else. Maybe it's a hormone you have, or an enzyme. Maybe it's got something to do with your brain structure. Something in your blood. Your cells might be unusual, or your DNA. It might be genetic, or it might come from your environment. We just don't know."

Abby glanced at Ben. He was listening hard, but she couldn't read his expression.

"But imagine if we *did*," said Phil. "Imagine if we could tap into whatever it is that makes you special, and bring it to the masses. Inside your special hormones, or your special

234

magnetism, or your special brain chemistry, might be the key to fantastic new drugs. Imagine a pill that would help athletes win more medals. Imagine if you could eat anything and never get fat, or if there were a spray that could heal any wound—or if we could figure out how to live forever! We just don't know yet. But if you'll help us out, we could bring happiness to so many people. Make people well. Make people better."

"And make a lot of money for your company," Ben concluded. "That's really the point, isn't it?"

Phil didn't appreciate that remark. "Yes, there will be a lot of money. Every company tries to make money. But we intend to share that money with you, Ben, and Abby, and the other kids—of course we do. You are the ones who will make it all possible, after all."

Phil had given a great speech, but Abby was feeling more annoyed than anything. "So if this is all so noble and so great, why are you keeping it all a secret? Why go to all the trouble of building a national chain of magic camps, just to find the kids who have powers?"

Phil smiled. "Well, we couldn't just come out and advertise what we're really doing, could we? 'Kids! Got a special power that seems pointless? Friends make fun of you? Come to our labs where we can study you, examine you, and run you through our machines!' I don't think many parents would sign up for that program. And besides . . . that would tell the other big pharma companies what we're up to. And we can't have that, can we?"

Abby looked down at her lap.

"Look, Abby . . . Ben. I know this is a lot to handle. But we've been working on this project for years, ever since we first became aware that there were these specially gifted children. You have the power to help so many people. To save lives. And maybe, if you're the kid who leads us to discovering your secret, to make a lot of money. Won't you just stay for one more week, so we can have our Level 2 researchers look you over? It's just a few days of . . . discomfort, in exchange for the possibility of helping us find a huge medical breakthrough. Can I count on you?"

Abby and Ben didn't believe Phil for a second. They knew perfectly well that he wasn't really giving them a choice; he had no intention of letting them go home before he was ready. If they were going to get out of there, it would have to be without Phil's help—and the first step would be to play along.

"Okay, Phil," Ben said, standing up. "Just a few more days."

"Thank you," said Phil. "And do we also have an understanding that this program needs to remain a secret? If you told anyone, like your parents or even the other kids here, it could destroy everything we've worked so hard to build here. Do we have a deal?"

Ben nodded.

"You, too, Abby?"

Her heart wasn't in it, but she nodded anyway.

"Okay, then," Phil concluded. "Enough serious stuff. You've missed half an hour of morning class already. Why don't I have Ferd take you back to the labs? And I'll see to it that a special yummy surprise is delivered to your rooms tonight, as my way of thanking you for your understanding."

I understand, all right, Abby thought, boiling with anger. *What I understand is that we're all just a bunch of South American ferns to you. We're the next big drug in your pipeline. We're the miracle cure that's gonna make you a billionaire. And to get us here, you tricked our parents, you tricked us—you tricked everybody.*

Well, you know what, Mr. Phil? The next trick's on you.

Sent: July 7
From: acarnelia11@gmail.com
To: eastportmama@optonline.net
Subject: Yo

Dear Ryan,

Remember me? The sister you adore? First kid in

237

our family? Word up, baby brother! (Code for "How are you, Ry?")

They are treating me great here. Are you having fun at home? Keeping busy? Me, I'm busier than a beaver! Prisoner of happiness, that's me!

This is a great trick I learned. Place a quarter on the table. Is it heads up? Really concentrate now. A picture should form in your mind, and you should say this chant. "Medicine man, witch doctor, evil eye! Company of wizards, make it FLY!"

They say that if you did it right, the quarter should drop right through the table. Are you seeing that, or did I explain it wrong? Editing the instructions might help, if I get time. My writing is not so great. E-mail is not so great for explaining magic tricks, either!

Can you believe I'll be home in a week? You betcha! Pick a day that weekend for going to see a movie or something. Me, I don't care what it is. Up here at camp, we see lots of movies, but it's not the same without you!

Look at the time—I gotta go. Up late again,
and I need to rest for tomorrow's fun activities.
Calabra Camps are the best—you should come
next year, Ryan!

Love,
Abs

CHAPTER
22
Escape

BY NOW, ABBY HAD FIGURED OUT why her parents had been responding so weirdly to her e-mails: somebody at Calabra was intercepting every single e-mail message. Reading them over, editing them, changing them, cutting out sentences from the kids' e-mails that might make parents suspicious, and anything from the parents' replies that showed worry.

No wonder no phones are allowed. No wonder every room has this super-fancy laptop in it, she thought. *It's set up so that they can fix up our e-mails before they go on their way!*

Every day, whenever she passed through the lobby, she had seen Candi, sitting there at her reception desk and tapping, tapping, tapping away on her computer. Now Abby wondered if that was part of Candi's job, to read over the e-mails and cut out anything that might reveal Calabra's secret.

After the lab, Abby hadn't gone to lunch; she told Ferd that she wasn't feeling well. Instead, she'd gone back to her room and woken up the laptop. She had a way to send e-mail that she was pretty sure would get right by Candi the E-mail Spy: she used the first-word code that Ryan had taught her.

She read it back to herself, to make sure that all the first words of the sentences made sense. "Remember The First Word Code? They Are Keeping Me Prisoner! This Place Is Really A Medicine Company. They Are Editing My E-mail! Can You Pick Me Up? Look Up 'Calabra.'"

She was pretty sure that Candi wouldn't find anything to cut out of it; unless you knew the code, it sounded pretty innocent. All but the word "Calabra." But maybe Candi would just think that was a typing mistake. Abby hoped so, anyway.

The next step: figuring out a way to get out of this place. When Abby really thought about it, the whole thing seemed hopeless. You needed a key card to open any of the doors. Even if you had one, you had to get past Candi at the reception desk. Or you could go at night when she was gone, but then the motion detectors and the pressure

241

sensors in the floors would set off the alarms. And that's if the guys in the black shirts didn't see you trying to escape first.

And even if they got out of the building complex—then what? Where would they go? They were miles from anywhere.

Ben. He'll know what to do.

She decided to go find him in the cafeteria. Lunch wasn't over yet—a good thing. Abby suddenly realized she was starving.

❧

"Why do we have to sit *here*, anyway?" Ricky yelled. "I'm getting splattered!"

"Yeah, seriously," muttered Eliza as loudly as it's possible to mutter. They sat side by side on the concrete rim of the courtyard fountain. Ben was standing. Abby was pacing.

"Because the fountain is so loud, nobody's gonna hear us," Abby yelled back. There was a pause, as everyone spontaneously listened to the roar of the water for a moment.

"All right, look. Let's say we believe you," Eliza finally said. She had pulled her hands inside the tentlike caverns of her T-shirt to keep warm, so she looked like a bizarre orange mannequin with no arms. "Let's say these guys are trying to turn us into their next miracle drug. I don't like what they're doing, and I don't like how they're doing it. But get *real*, Abby. You really think we can get out of here? This place is locked up like Fort Knox!"

Ricky looked at her. "What's Fort Knox?"

Eliza scoffed at him. "It's just a saying, numbskull. It means it's really hard to get out of here."

"Listen, you guys! I have it mostly figured out," Abby announced. "We *can* get out of here if we all work together. But we need one of those security cards. After Ben set the alarms off the other night, they're probably being a lot more careful about locking the doors. That's the only part I haven't figured out. They all wear security cards like name tags on their shirts, or stuck in their wallets or purses. I can't think of any way to get our hands on one. One! That's all we need, and we can get out of this place!"

Ben was looking at her with a crooked smile. His floppy hair looked like it was practically right in his eyeballs; after two weeks of camp, he needed a haircut.

"All you need is a security card?"

She nodded. "That's the hard part."

"Wanna see a trick?"

"Are you kidding me? You're gonna do a magic trick right now?" she asked.

He held out his hands, empty, so she could see them. Then he turned them down toward the ground so she could see their backs. Then he put his hands together, like a sandwich.

"Abby Cadabra," he said. He peeled his hands apart.

There was a security card between them.

Abby clapped her hands despite herself, and Ricky's eyes were wide. "Hey! Where did you get that?"

"From Candi's desk. The key we used to open the desk door also opens the desk *drawer*. Handy, eh? She must keep this card in there as a spare." He shrugged. "I felt that I needed it more than she does."

"Ben! You're amazing," said Abby. She held her hand up for a high five; he slapped her palm.

"So when do we make our big escape?" asked Eliza.

"Are you kidding me? Tonight. I don't want to spend one single second hypnotized in some cat tube," said Abby.

Ben smiled. "You mean a CAT scan."

Abby turned to face the fountain. "I mean, we're outta here. Are you guys with me?"

She meant to ask that question the way a cheerleader would—she already knew the answer, but she wanted to hear them jump up with team spirit and yell, "YEAH!!"

But that wasn't the reaction she got.

"It's not going to work," Eliza said.

"I don't want to go home!" pleaded Ricky.

Abby couldn't believe it. "You don't want—Ricky, are you kidding me? Do you want them to poke you full of

244

needles and hypnotize you and knock you unconscious and cut open your brain?"

Ricky pouted and looked down at his feet.

"I like the remote-control helicopters," was all he said.

Abby shot Ben a *help-me-out-here!* look, her hands spread apart.

Ben put his hand on Ricky's shoulder. "Ricky, listen. I don't think they're going to let us do much more of the fun stuff after tomorrow," he said. He pulled the camper calendar from his back jeans pocket and unfolded it. "You're going to be in the hospital part of this camp. They want to find out how you got your power, and see if they can get it out of you. Like, with you strapped down to a table so you can't move. With needles and stuff. Is that what you want?"

Ricky, deeply upset, began to cry.

"Nice job there, Captain Persuasion," Eliza said to Ben dryly.

He shot her an irritated look.

"Ricky, Ricky . . . don't be scared," Ben said soothingly. "None of that's going to happen if you'll help us! Okay? In fact, I'll tell you what. Help us get out of here tonight, and then I will personally take you to go fly some helicopters once we get home, okay? Won't that be fun?"

Ricky nodded unhappily, wiping his nose with his sleeve.

"It's going to be fine. Why don't we let Abby tell us her

plan for getting us out of here? Let's listen to her idea, and then we'll talk about it. Okay?"

He reached around Ricky with both arms as though about to give him a hug, but at the last minute, he chickened out and just patted Ricky's back with both hands.

"All right," said Abby finally. "Listen carefully now, because for the rest of the day, we're gonna have to pretend that nothing's up. And if one little thing goes wrong . . ."

She looked at Ricky's quivering face and decided she'd better not finish that sentence. She had a lot of explaining to do—and a hard-boiled egg to swipe from the cafeteria.

Ricky and Eliza thought that Abby was crazy for wanting to escape from Camp Cadabra—or Calabra Pharmaceuticals, as they now knew it was called. But in the end, they agreed to join her.

They set their alarms for the middle of the night—"1:15 a.m. in the morning," as Eliza called it. Nobody liked that idea much, either, but slipping out after most of the Calabra workers were asleep definitely seemed like the best idea.

By 1:20 a.m., Abby, Ben, and Eliza were all together in the lobby, leaning on the desk where Candi usually sat. But there was no sign of Ricky.

"Where *is* he?" Abby whispered.

"Why are you asking me?" Eliza whispered back.

"I'll bet he's still sleeping," said Ben. "And I don't know how we're gonna wake him up without waking up everybody in the place."

The three of them crossed the lobby toward the short hallway to Ricky's room. They tried to knock on his door loudly enough to wake him, but gently enough not to get anyone's attention.

There was still no answer. Abby got on the floor to call his name under the door. "Come on guys, help me out," she said.

"*Riccckkkeeeeeee! Rickeeeeeee!*" they all hissed together, crouched on their hands and knees. "Wake up!!"

They were still there, their faces pressed against the doorsill, when the door flew open.

It was Ricky, yawning and blinking in his Spider-Man pajamas.

"What are you guys doing on the floor?"

"Come on! Get dressed," said Abby, standing up. "You were supposed to wake up and escape with us! Come on!"

Ricky worked his jaw up and down a few times, as though it were a little rusty. He rubbed his eyes. "What time is it?"

"We've gotta go, Rick," said Ben. "We need you to come with us! Can you hurry up and get dressed?"

Ten minutes later, the four campers were out in the lobby of their living pod, standing by the double doors that opened onto the hallway to freedom.

"Okay, so tell us again how we do this?" asked Eliza. For once, she wasn't wearing a T-shirt that was six sizes too big. She was wearing a *sweater* that was six sizes too big.

Abby took a breath. "Okay, well, remember, our first worry is the motion sensors. It's those little round lenses right inside the hallway doors. If they see any movement in the hallway, the metal gates are gonna come down, and we'll be trapped like mice. That would *not* be good! So as soon as the hallway doors open, Ricky, you fog 'em up, okay?"

"I what?" said Ricky, still not entirely awake.

"Ricky, we went over this before. Use your power! Can't you do that? Can't you fog up glass from far away?"

"Oh, yeah," said Ricky. "But I've never tried it on cameras."

"Well, guess what? Tonight's your lucky night. But first, we've got to open the doors to the hallway. Ben, this is you."

"Yes, captain," he said. He pulled Candi's spare key card from his pocket. All four kids stepped back so they'd be out of the way when the doors opened—and not visible to the motion cameras just inside the hallway.

Ben swiped the card across the black box by the door.

248

There was a click, and the doors swung outward into the hallway.

"Okay, Ricky!" Abby whispered. "Do your thing!"

Ricky peeked into the hallway and saw the small round lenses mounted near the floor, one on each side of the hallway. As quietly as he could, he did his Spanish counting-by-twos while breathing in (and it's not easy to do that quietly).

"*Dos, cuatro, seis, ocho, diez!*" he said.

The light was fairly dim, but Abby thought that she could see a silvery, misty reflection on the lens, which usually looked like a solid black circle. Ricky changed his focus to the lens on the opposite side and repeated his counting.

"I think he did it!" Abby said, beaming. "Good job, Ricky!"

Ricky beamed even more.

"So what now?" asked Eliza. If anyone in the world could actually act bored during a panicky, late-night escape from a secret scientific laboratory, it was Eliza.

"Now we have to get to the other end of the hallway," Abby said. "The problem is the floor. It's pressure-sensitive, you guys. If you step on it, then you set off the alarm. This is all you, Eliza."

"Yeah, great," said Eliza. She had never been a fan of this part of Abby's scheme. "Couldn't we just pole vault?"

"Come on, Eliza," chided Ben. "Be a good sport. And quick, before those lenses unfog."

Eliza had never been good at being a good sport. "Okay, first of all, I'm not your trained dog. I don't levitate on command. Second of all, I told you: this isn't going to work. I can't balance when I'm levitating. It's like standing on marbles. I tip right over."

"Please, Eliza. I know you don't do it on command; we're *asking* you. There's not going to be any way across that floor without you. And unless we get across that floor, we're staying here another week!"

"Eliza, please," said Ben.

"Yeah! I used my power," added Ricky with pride.

Eliza crossed her arms. "Well, I can't balance."

Abby nodded. "I've been thinking about that. I was wondering if you'd ever tried levitating, you know . . . on your back?"

"On my back? Are you—That is the dumbest idea I ever heard!"

There was an uncomfortable silence. And it took Ricky to break it. "Why is that dumb? That way, you wouldn't fall down. You'd already be down!"

"It's going to work, Eliza!" said Abby, giving it one last try. "Look: you lie down, just like you're on a towel on the beach, okay? You're levitating just a tiny bit off the ground.

We give your feet a little push, and you glide across to the other side. That's it! If you touch the floor a little here and there, it's not gonna matter; the alarm only goes off if somebody is *walking* on it. Please, Eliza. We *need* you!"

Eliza sighed and looked into the hallway. "Well, it's never gonna work, but apparently you need to see that for yourself. Where do you want me?"

"Oh, you're awesome, Eliza," Ben said. Abby and Ricky tried to offer her high fives, but Eliza wasn't interested.

"Okay, so, sort of lie down with your arms out, right here," Abby said, indicating a spot right at the opening of the hallway.

Eliza lay down. "Okay, now what?"

"Come on, guys, help me out!" whispered Abby, squatting down by Eliza's feet. We'll have to give her a little push!"

The two boys kneeled and put their hands on Eliza's sneakers.

"Aim her straight, you guys. Eliza, are you ready?"

"Let's get it over with," came the reply.

"Okay, Eliza. Now—you know—rise up! Think about those buffalos," Abby said.

"Walking backward," added Ben.

"Wearing diapers!" Ricky reminded her, giggling with glee.

"I know how to do it!" Eliza snapped.

If you were right down next to her, with your head against the floor, you might have been able to see that her whole body had lifted off the floor by just the tiniest little bit—about the height of a chocolate bar.

"Okay, guys!" said Abby. "One, two—"

"Wait!" said Ricky. "The camera! It's not fogged up anymore!"

It was true. The silvery sheen on the motion detector had almost completely evaporated.

"Well, juice it up again, will you?" Eliza said, a little bit crankily.

"Would you mind re-fogging it, Ricky?" said Abby. "Keep checking it, too. We can't afford to let it unfog until we're out of here."

Ricky did his Spanish counting thing again, fogged the camera, and then got ready to push.

"All right, let's try this again," said Abby. "Eliza, you up?"

"I'm up," she said.

"All right, here we go: One, two, three—push!"

Abby, Ben, and Ricky pushed against Eliza's feet. Of course, they had no idea how hard to push; they had had very little practice launching eleven-year-old levitating girls down hallways.

If you tried to push a normal person across the floor,

you'd have to push very hard, because the person's body would rub against the carpet and not go very far at all. But if somebody were lying on a big skateboard, you wouldn't have to push nearly as hard. And if there were nothing between the person and the floor but air, you wouldn't have to push very hard at all.

But they realized that too late. They pushed Eliza much too hard. Her body, with her arms out like a T, zipped across the floor like a roller coaster going downhill. Her sweater dragged on the floor a little, and she wobbled enough to scrape the tiles—not enough to trigger the alarm. But before she even realized what was going on, she had reached the doors at the far end of the hallway—with her head.

WHACK!

"OW!" she yelled, thumping to the floor. She sat up, rubbing her head. "Jeez, you people! What are you trying to do, kill me?"

The three other kids apologized, sincerely and as loudly as they could while still whispering. "I'm sorry, Eliza!" "We didn't know!" "Are you okay?"

Eliza, now safely on the part of the floor that wasn't wired to the alarm, glared at them for another minute, then turned around and pushed the far doors open. She could see the long, carpeted hallway that led to the building's main lobby—but suddenly she stopped.

"Wait—now what? Do I just go? How do you guys get over here?"

Ricky and Ben turned to Abby with an expectant look on their faces, ready for the next instruction. There was only one problem: Abby didn't have one to give them.

"I—I didn't think about this part," she admitted.

"Well, great," Eliza said.

"Is there a button over there, Eliza?" said Ben. "Something that turns off the floor?" He had seen Phil and other people walk that hallway without triggering any alarm, so he knew there must be a way to turn off the floor's pressure sensitivity. But whatever the control was, Eliza couldn't find it.

Eliza poked around the far walls and the double doors. She shook her head no. "Nothing here," she said.

"Maybe we should go back to bed?" said Ricky hopefully.

"No, no, come on, you guys," said Abby.

"Maybe I should just escape," Eliza offered. "And I'll find a way to come back for you."

"No!" said the other three, all together.

"We've come this far," Abby added. "We can figure this out!"

"I don't know, Abby," Ben said softly. "Only Eliza can get across the floor without sounding the alarm. I don't see how the rest of us are gonna get across."

"You're right," said Abby, suddenly confident. "Only Eliza can get across." She turned. "Eliza! You have to come back!"

Eliza, now with a very sore bump on the top of her head, was not thrilled. "What are you *talking* about? I'm already across!"

"You have to come back. It's the only way," Abby said.

"Who's gonna push me?"

"Just push with your feet. Kick off from the door frame."

"And what then? What happens once I'm back over there?"

"I'll tell you once you get here!"

With an enormous sigh, Eliza lay down at the far end of the hallway, levitated herself, and gave herself a push. She glided smoothly across the floor and coasted to a stop—three feet from the end of the hallway.

"Help!" she hissed, desperately trying to keep the image of buffalo in her head.

Ben fell to his knees and reached out with his hand, but she was a few inches too far away.

"Maybe your leg?" said Abby.

Ben sat down, leaned back on his elbows, and stretched his feet out toward Eliza. He couldn't reach her armpits, but he managed to hook the toe of one shoe under her chin—and gave her a tug.

"Eewww!" said Eliza, despite herself. She sailed to the safe part of the floor just as she forgot to think of the buffalos—and she scraped down for a landing.

"Did you have to stick your stinky foot in my face?"

Ben stood up, brushing off his pants. "Well, actually, kind of yeah. Either that or leave you floating in the hallway until we all get caught."

Clearly, this was not Eliza's favorite morning. And it was about to get worse.

"All right," she said to Abby. "Now I'm back. What's your bright idea?"

"Now, I know you're not gonna like this," Abby said as respectfully as she could. "I just want you to know that you're really the hero, Eliza. You're making this possible by generously using your power to get us out of here."

"Yeah, yeah, whatever. What's your idea?"

Abby took a breath. "Okay. Well, is there any weight limit to your power? I mean, could it carry you *and* someone else?"

Suddenly, Eliza understood where Abby was going.

"Oohhhhhh, no you don't," she said, waving her hands in front of her face. "I am not going to float down that hallway with you guys sitting on top of me. No way. Forget it. I'm not some stinking flying carpet!"

The funny thing was, when she had floated across the

hallway floor, wearing that huge floppy sweater, Eliza had actually looked a lot like a flying carpet.

"Won't you consider it?" said Ben. "You're our only hope."

"Yeah," said Ricky. "Please?"

"When they write the history books, you'll be the one who saved the day," Abby added.

Eliza glared at them. "You're all ganging up on me!"

"We're just asking," said Abby gently.

Finally, Eliza gave a grunt of frustration—sort of a "HhhrrreeeeaAAAAAGHHH!!"—and lay down on her back again. "All right. But you people owe me big time." She spread her arms out.

Abby didn't give Eliza a chance to change her mind. "Okay, Ricky. You first. Climb up."

After some fumbling, they figured out that the best way to ride was to sit on Eliza's stomach, facing forward. Ricky rested his feet on her shoulders; he leaned back so that his hands gripped her ankles. It looked and felt a lot like sledding, actually—at least to Ricky.

To Eliza, it was pure discomfort. "All right, let's get this over with," she muttered. She closed her eyes and lifted slightly off the floor. Fortunately, magic doesn't care about weight or mass; Eliza discovered that levitating with Ricky was no more difficult than levitating without him.

"Okay, Ben. Help me push," said Abby.

"Not so hard this time!" Eliza hissed.

"We know, we know," said Ben. "Ricky—stop her with your feet."

Ben and Abby realized that they didn't dare push Eliza *too* lightly, because then she'd be stranded in the middle of the hallway with nobody to pull her to safety. So on the count of three, they gave Eliza a decent shove down the hallway.

She sailed across the floor; it was all Ricky could do not to shout "Yee-haw!" Just as she was about to thud against the far door, Ricky stuck his feet forward to act as bumpers, so Eliza didn't crack her head again.

It actually worked out pretty well. Ricky was safely across.

Then it was Abby's turn. As she scooched onto Eliza's stomach, she pulled the hard-boiled egg from her pocket and handed it back to Ben. "Hold this a minute," she said.

"What's this for?" he said, mystified.

"Insurance."

In another minute, Eliza had ferried Abby across, too. But Ben was a problem; since he was the last one to go, there was nobody to push Eliza down the hallway.

There was, however, a thin handrail on the side of the

hallway. In the end, Ben had the bright idea of pulling himself along the railing, hand over hand, basically dragging Eliza along with him.

It was quite a sight: a sixth-grade girl, floating on her back, her multicolored floppy sweater spread out like a bat's wings; a skinny fourteen-year-old boy sitting on her stomach as though on a toboggan, dragging himself along a handrail; a short, round-headed kid at the end of the hallway, jumping up and down and occasionally counting by twos in Spanish to keep the security cameras fogged up; and Abby, chewing the ends of her shiny dark hair out of pure nerves.

When Ben and Eliza were halfway across, Abby began yell-whispering to him. "Ben! Put the egg down, okay? Just put it in the middle of the floor as you go by! Set it down!"

Ben paused, baffled, one hand on the railing, and set the egg down in the hallway. Then he continued tugging his floating girl barge along the wall.

It wasn't pretty, and it wasn't quick. But finally, all four kids had reached the end of the hallway.

Only a few seconds later, they were running through the lobby they had entered the day they arrived, fogging security cameras as they ran.

At last, at 2:11 a.m., they burst out through the front

doors into the cool summer night. They stood panting just outside the building, deliriously proud and happy that their plan had worked.

Then they heard the click—and were blasted by lights and sound.

CHAPTER
23
Gates

THE ALARMS WENT OFF a fraction of a second after all the lights came on—lights both inside and outside the Calabra building.

Ben was the first to come to his senses. "They heard us!" he shouted.

"Oh, no!" shrieked Ricky, completely panicked.

"It's over," muttered Eliza. "Figures."

"It's not over," Abby said. "You guys—get going up the hill. Run out to the road at the top. I'll be there in a second."

"What are you gonna do?" asked Ben. "If you stay here, they're going to catch you!"

"No, they're not," Abby said. "For once in my life, I think

my dumb little power might actually be useful. Now get going! I mean it!"

"I agree," intoned Eliza. "If she wants to get caught, fine. But I'm outta here." And she started up the hill. Ricky and Ben reluctantly trotted after her.

Abby suddenly felt incredibly alone. The little insurance-policy idea that had seemed so smart a few minutes ago suddenly seemed risky and foolish.

But she took a breath and ran back into the building. She stopped just at the beginning of the motion-sensor hall-way, which was already echoing with the sound of excited men's voices approaching from inside the building.

Abby scanned the hallway floor until she spotted the little white dot she was looking for—the egg that Ben had left there. She backed slowly away, hoping to get as far away as possible and still keep her eyes on that egg. If all the lights hadn't been on, it might have been hard to spot; but as it was, Abby could see it even from halfway into the front lobby.

These days Abby can't tell you whether one minute or one second passed before she saw the black-shirted secu-rity men burst into view at the far end of the hallway; with all the buzzing and blinking and pounding in her ears, time turned into a hopeless knot.

One thing she knew for sure: she had to activate the

motion sensors before the men could reach the control box to turn them off. And the way to do that was to spin the egg.

Abby had never, ever attempted to spin an egg from so far away. And she had no idea if it would work.

She tugged her ears. For the first second, nothing happened—but then, the egg, so far away that it was barely visible, actually began to spin. The motion cameras saw movement at floor level and did what they were designed to do, just as Abby had desperately hoped: they triggered the metal gates at both ends of the hallway.

The guards arrived at the far end of the hallway just in time to see the metal gates clattering down from the ceiling. Some of them were swearing and shouting and grabbing the metal gate to stop it from reaching the floor. But the gate motors were too strong.

"TURN IT OFF! TURN THE DARN THING OFF!" shouted a familiar voice. It sounded like Kermit the Frog having a really bad day.

"I'm trying, all right? Calm yourself, for the love of Peter!" That was Ferd's voice—the last one Abby heard, echoing down the corridor, as she bolted for the front lobby.

Ferd fumbled at the control panel. He turned a key. He slapped two illuminated buttons to shut off the sensors. He waited with the others for the metal gates to open again. He ran with them down the deactivated hallway toward the front entrance.

But Abby had done what she wanted to do: gained a four-minute head start for her friends.

By the time Ferd, Phil Shutter, and the guards made it out of the building, Abby was halfway up the broad grassy slope of the Calabra valley—halfway to rejoining Ben, Eliza, and Ricky, who had almost reached the street.

CHAPTER
24
Hitchhikers

As you probably know, Abby didn't write this book herself. It's her story, of course, and what you're reading here is pretty much the way she tells it. But she didn't write this book—I did. And it's only fair to tell you how I got involved.

I was driving through Pennsylvania on my way home from a business meeting one night—really, really late at night. I was getting so sleepy, I thought I should stop somewhere and get some coffee. And that's why I was driving more slowly than usual on the highway at about 2:30 in the morning.

Suddenly, in my headlights, I saw a little clump of junior high school–age kids standing on the side of the road.

They were jumping up and down, waving their arms to flag me down. They seemed pretty frantic about it; something was obviously wrong.

So I steered my Prius onto the side of the road and pulled up a few yards away. These crazy kids came running over to the car. I rolled down the window.

"You kids all right?" I asked.

They were all talking at once, and panting hard at the same time, so it was a little hard to figure out exactly what they wanted. But finally, the girl with the dark hair shushed the other kids and spoke directly to me.

"We need a ride, and we need to use your cell phone," she said, out of breath. "It's really, *really* important. Please. *Please*. We just ran all the way up the hill from way down there."

The tall boy spoke up, again with incredible urgency in his voice. "We're being chased! Can you help us? *Please?*"

I have to admit, this didn't seem right to me at all. I had no idea what these guys were running away from. For all I knew, they had just busted out of kiddie jail. I didn't want to get in trouble by helping them.

"What are you running away from?"

"Them!" said the redheaded girl in the huge sweater, pointing down the long grassy hill. For the first time, I could see moving flashlights coming up from the bottom

266

of the hill. I could just hear voices shouting and a couple of car engines starting up, too. "They're going to want to capture us back. *Please, sir!*"

"Look," I said. "I'd love to help you, I really would. But I could be arrested for kidnapping you!"

The dark-haired girl—of course, it was Abby—put her hands on my car window frame and spoke intensely.

"We don't have time to explain this," she said. "We just want to get back to our parents!"

The men's voices from the hill were getting louder.

Abby suddenly seemed to have a new idea. "Listen: If you're worried about being arrested, then why don't you drive us straight to a police station? That way, you don't have to worry. If we're running away from jail, they'll put us right back in. And if we're telling the truth, then the police will help us get back home! Okay?"

The whole business sounded crazy to me. But I had to admit, her logic was pretty solid. Besides—every now and then, you've got to listen to your gut. Meanwhile, the voices, lights, and cars were getting closer, fast.

"All right," I said. "Get in."

Three of the kids climbed in back, and the oldest one sat in front. They closed the doors. Two men's voices were shouting at me from only fifty yards away. If I waited about three more seconds, I'd be able to make out what they were saying.

267

But I didn't. I drove. I had no idea where to find a police station in the middle of the night in a strange part of the country, but I figured I could pull into a gas station to ask.

"What are your names?"

They told me. Ricky asked me my name, and what I did for work.

"I'm David," I answered. "I write for the *New York Times*."

"Oh . . . my . . . gosh," said Abby, behind me. "I think you're exactly the person we need to talk to."

And that's how it happened. That's how I got to know Abby Carnelia: driving along a deserted Pennsylvania highway in the middle of the night.

They told me everything during that dark ride, overlapping, shouting, interjecting: about the summer camps around the country, about these one-in-a-thousand children with their useless little powers, about the giant company that was trying to pick them apart and turn them into the sources of the next billion-dollar drug. It all sounded like farfetched fiction to me. Yet their details were so precise, and their stories fit together so perfectly, that I grew increasingly curious.

They took turns using my cell phone to call their parents. You want to know the most amazing part of the whole thing? Abby's parents were only about 45 minutes away. Apparently, they had received an e-mail message from her that day, did a little research on Calabra, and piled into the family car to rescue her. They'd already been driving for hours.

In the end, they met us at the police station in Moroville, Pennsylvania, in the wee—*very wee*—hours of the morning. It was all happy chaos: Mrs. Carnelia wrapped her arms around Abby like an octopus and wouldn't let go; she just kept chanting, "Oh, Abby. Oh, Abby. Oh, Abby." Mr. Carnelia threw his arms around them both, spinning the whole group around and around. Ryan waited anxiously for his turn, standing nearby until there was hugging room.

"You did the code!" he shouted, his face lit up. "You did the code! Mom showed it to me and I knew how to read it! It really worked, right, Ab? It really worked!"

Since Abby's father was an airline pilot, he was able to arrange flights for the other parents so they could pick up their kids in the morning.

There was food to be ordered, and hotel rooms to be booked, and a *whole* lot of explaining to do.

But by 7:00 a.m., I had already spoken to my editor at the newspaper, and I knew my next step: I needed to pay a little visit to Calabra Pharmaceuticals. Something told me that there was quite a story waiting to be written for the paper.

Or maybe even a book.

CHAPTER
25
Afterward

"I'M CHAD FRESNO, and this . . . is *Been There, Done That!*"

The studio audience cheered wildly for as long as the little man with the headset ran around waving the AP-PLAUSE sign back and forth.

Chad Fresno, Abby noticed, was what her dad called a "three-lumper." His hair looked like three carefully frozen, shiny lumps of plastic: one on top, one on each side of his head. He sat down in the swiveling leather chair across from Abby on the mini-stage.

"Every week, we introduce you to someone who's lived an experience that the rest of us encounter only in our dreams—or our nightmares," he said to the TV camera. "And today, we bring you a young lady we've plucked right out of the headlines." Abby smiled, but her stomach had turned to nervous Jell-O.

The chance to appear on national TV had seemed like it would be really cool—and it *had* been cool, especially when a limousine had arrived to pick up the Carnelias and take them to New York City for the show.

The bright TV lights made it hard to see any faces in the audience, but Abby knew that her family was out there. So was her best friend, Morgan, who had insisted on coming along in case Abby needed a bodyguard. Even No-H Sara had made the trip to the city to see Abby's big TV moment.

"It's been in all the papers, it's been all over the Internet: last week, police raided the Pennsylvania headquarters of Calabra Pharmaceuticals," Chad was saying to the camera. "Inside, they found twenty-one children being held virtually prisoner, far from home and facing medical experimentation against their will. Calabra, we now know, had built a chain of five summer camps as a sort of hunting ground for kids with special abilities."

On the TV monitors, Abby could see video being played back. It showed a bunch of police cars driving down the long, sloping driveway of Calabra's valley headquarters, lights flashing. There was a shot of Phil being escorted out of the building by two officers, and even a glimpse of what

Abby thought she recognized as Ferd's ponytail bouncing along in the group behind.

"Today on *Been There, Done That*, we welcome a very special guest: the young lady who first uncovered the scheme and helped bring Calabra Pharmaceuticals to justice. Please help me welcome seventh grader Abby Carnelia!"

There was cheering and applause. Abby shoved her hair behind her ears nervously.

Chad turned at last to face her. She noticed for the first time that he was wearing makeup. "Abby, tell us: how has your life changed since you got home from Calabra?"

"Well, it's been a little crazy," Abby said. Her voice came out strangely at first, but her confidence grew as she spoke. "There are still news people camped out across the street from our house. They take pictures when we leave the house, and they shout my name and stuff. I've had to do a lot of interviews. And once when I went to the pool, some of my friends from school wanted my autograph. That was cool."

The audience chuckled.

"They're calling you a hero, Abby. Did you ever think you'd be called a hero?"

Abby looked down for a moment, shaking her head.

"I'm not sure I deserve that," she said. "Because there were four of us. We kind of figured out what was going on together, and broke out of there together."

Chad nodded knowingly. "Have you been in touch with your friends from Calabra?"

Abby shook her head no. "It's been too crazy."

"Well, Abby, we *have* been in touch with them. And I think it's time to introduce them to the whole world. Ladies and gentlemen, please welcome to the stage, Ben, Ricky, and Eliza!"

Abby's jaw dropped in surprise. She'd had no idea that this TV show would be a reunion. But sure enough, here came Ricky, his very round head bobbing as he stepped onto the stage; Eliza, wearing a T-shirt dress that was much too big for her; and finally, Ben, loping amiably into the lights.

Abby ran forward to greet them. There was a massive group hug in the middle of the set, and so much excited babbling that Chad had to break them up.

"We do have a TV show to do here, guys," he kidded them.

Ben, Ricky, and Eliza sat down in the chairs next to Abby's. She was beaming, delighted to see them again.

"All right then," Chad said finally. He rotated his chair to face his four guests. "I want to hear the whole story. Who wants to start?"

The best part of the TV show wasn't the actual interview; in fact, Abby found that nerve-racking. No, the best part came afterward, when the four middle-school musketeers got to gab and catch up and remember their adventure. The four families spent two days romping through New York and having fun.

Mr. and Mrs. Carnelia couldn't help noticing that Abby was especially happy to see Ben again. So they invited Ben and his parents to come spend a few days in Connecticut at the end of the summer. It wasn't like Ben was, you know, Abby's *boyfriend* or anything. But they'd been through so much together, and had become so close, that Abby knew they'd be friends forever.

It was the biggest science news in years: the discovery of a rare, very special breed of children who can bend the laws of nature—in tiny, pointless ways.

Actually, everybody *thought* these were rare, very special children. But Abby Carnelia wasn't quite finished.

You see, ever since she saw Ben discover a power of his own, she hadn't been able to stop thinking: *What's the difference between Ben, before he discovered his power, and every other kid in the world? Nothing at all.*

Every kid who's ever had a power started out as someone who didn't have a power. And the only way people discover their magic is by accident—by stumbling onto whatever the freaky trigger might be. The conditions have to be exactly right, or it won't happen.

There has to be, you know, a hard-boiled egg sitting on the counter when you tug on your earlobes.

Abby realized that there might be a lot of kids who have powers—but who just haven't discovered them yet. They may be everywhere.

In fact—and this is the part that blew Abby's mind—they could be *everyone.*

For all she knew, every single person in the world might have a little magic inside, some freaky little ability. Including every one of her friends, and even strangers.

And even you.

The question was, how could she help people find their magic?

Find Your Magic started as an after-school club. Every Tuesday afternoon, kids would come in and experiment. They'd bring in all kinds of props and objects: balls, crayons, coins, shoes, liquids, papers, toys, aluminum foil, Silly Putty, buttons, Cheetos, rulers, cardboard, rubber bands, M&Ms . . . all kinds of stuff.

And then they'd try to find their triggers. They'd try everything they could think of: flapping, singing, dancing, waving, breathing, blinking, jumping, thinking, scratching, tugging, wiggling, burping, clapping, slapping, chomping, pressing, gulping, flicking, singing, bending, eating, snapping—always hoping to find something that had an unexpected effect.

One day, in the spring, near the end of seventh grade, someone did. A kid found his power. It was a boy from Abby's history class. He managed to make everyone else in the room hear a high, very faint violin note—or think they heard one—when he put a quarter between his toes.

There was no violin, of course, and no actual sound; you couldn't record it. But everyone in the room would swear that there was a sound. Abby had helped her first student find his power.

It caused such a sensation that the first Abby Carnelia's Find-Your-Magic Center opened six months later, in a shopping mall about two miles from Abby's house. At this point, almost everyone knew who Abby Carnelia was, so kids begged their parents to sign up for time at the center.

Now anyone could play with all those feathers, Slinkies, socks, marbles, lipstick tubes, cloth scraps, grapes, Popsicle sticks, Lego bricks, toothpicks, marshmallows, paper clips, clocks, twist-ties, hats, spoons, and hard-boiled eggs, trying every trigger that Abby and her workers suggested, in hopes of finding their magic. Eventually, somebody always did, and the word spread.

For a while, even adults sometimes stopped in to try. But they never seemed to find their magic; Abby eventually came to believe that if you don't find your magic while you're still a kid, it goes away.

Even so, in no time at all, there were Find-Your-Magic Centers all over the country. Nowadays, even kids who are too young to remember how it all began say, " 'Bye mom! I'm going to Abby's!" And they ride their bikes over to a center after school.

Now, I won't lie to you; most kids never do find out what their power is. After all, the chances are very small that you'll find the right trigger under the right circumstances.

But nobody seems to mind. People have fun trying to find their powers. And most of all, it's a great feeling just to know that you're special—even if you never do find out exactly why.